THE LIMBIC HIGHWAY

(our galactic connection)

PHILIP MCINERNEY

ISBN: 0982468504
ISBN 13: 9780982468500
Library of Congress Control Number: 2014907592
Saunal Publishing Incorporated, Kailua, Hawaii

ONE

Timeline: Ten Years Ago

Jake Martee is enjoying his tenth birthday party with family and friends at C's Pizza Parlor. He stuffs himself with pizza, hot dogs, garlic fries, sodas, popcorn, chocolate cake, candy, and ice cream.

After the party, the family plans to watch a video together, and when they arrive home, they find a freshly baked peanut butter honey cream pie, which Auntie Tianna dropped off earlier. The pie is Jake's favorite, and during the movie, he has two slices and a large glass of cold milk.

During the film, he starts to feel sick and begins coughing, tossing and turning on the couch, his stomach painfully full of too wide an assortment of ingredients.

Jake's mom goes to the medicine cabinet for something to calm her son. The cough syrup for kids is nearly empty, so she mixes what is left with a few teaspoons of her husband John's prescription elixir. The label is worn, and she does not realize her husband's cough syrup is laced with codeine. Jake has one and a half teaspoons, and then dozes a bit during the movie. When the movie ends around nine thirty, Dad has to wake his three children and send them to bed. Jake makes his way to his room and throws himself onto his bed. Fortunately he put his pajamas on earlier so he could just pass out from exhaustion.

But in bed, Jake feels even worse. He sweats hard, while his head swims with hallucinations. He has never experienced anything like this feeling. Garlic,

1

chocolate, and peanut butter, topped off with codeine, have combined into a toxic poison in his young system. His heart is pounding, and his blood is nearly boiling. His brain is racing terribly, seething with disturbing questions, scary thoughts, and devilish influence.

"What is happening?" he thinks. "I don't feel good."

He feels himself drift off into an abyss, frightened as never before. He dives haphazardly, deeper and deeper, toward a black, horrifying, bottomless pit. He tries desperately to avoid its pull, but drifts downward, as powerless as a cinder on the wind.

Now scenes of his young life flash in front of him. His mother and father are smiling, looking happily down upon him in his crib. "Mom!" he cries.

Next, he is in the kitchen, laughing and playing with Jon and Jan, his brother and sister. Jake reaches high in the cupboard to pilfer the hidden chocolate bars Mom has stashed away. "Be careful, Jake. That's Mom's favorite cookie jar!" warns Jan. He grabs the candy and turns toward Jan—but now, he is with his friends. They are pleading with him to keep up with them as they speed off on their bicycles away from trouble, but he cannot keep up. The strong pull of the abyss keeps him from being heard, and it will not allow his legs to pedal faster.

Now he sees his family in church, crying out loud. "Why would this happen to our Jake?" he hears them cry. The light in the church where his family goes to pray grows dimmer as Jake falls closer to the bottom.

"No!" he yells. "I'm over here—can't you hear me? Mom!"

Jake wants badly to get out of his nightmare, but the villainous grip will not let go. He feels all the pains from his short life fester. His ankle throbs from the time he got his foot caught in the spokes of his dad's bicycle. The terrible bruise deep in his thigh, acquired from running into a pipe in an alley near the welder's shop, aches like it just happened. He feels the strong humility of embarrassing Robin Stetts during the second grade, as her face flashes in front of him.

Now he is clinging to hanging stairs that descend the cliff-like wall of the abyss. He can see the bottom rungs of the stairs swaying and then disappearing into the depths of nothing. He tries to grab the side of the cliff, but the stairs won't stay still enough to let him get a hold. Darkness is trying to capture the entire atmosphere.

Jake tries with all his might to move upward, toward the remaining good light. Everything around him is getting hot and uncomfortable. He clenches his teeth and tightens his muscles with all his might. He attempts, over and over again, to grab hold of anything to help him avoid the pull of the darkness below, but to no avail. He feels like a fly in a spider's web, frantically trying to escape horrific clutches, only to calmly resign after losing his strength and will. He feels like giving up and is slowly sinking into the shadows below. In his apathy, he does not even realize he has wet the bed. His body is succumbing to the devil's wishes.

Suddenly, surprisingly, Jake's brain levels and cools, and he feels himself moving away from the swirling descent. He sees a face in the clouds looking at him. The face is kind, gentle, loving, smiling, and peaceful. In an instant, he is floating on a field of clouds, gaining altitude in the opposite direction from the dreaded darkness. With a surge of joy and inspiration, he feels his heart beating strongly in his chest.

He hears a soothing male voice. "You will be OK, my son!"

The pressure within his skull and the pounding of his heart subside. He falls into a deep sleep, safe in the confines of his own bed.

In the morning, Jake awakens drenched in sweat. He smells like a combination of garlic, peanut butter, urine, and toxins. He gets up, changes his pajamas, goes to the window, opens it, and takes large breaths of fresh air. A colorful, quiet sunrise blankets the sky. He feels the heavens in his heart. "I have been saved from the devil's grip," he thinks. So it is.

TWO

Timeline: Current

Blink and Dawne Owen's parents are away for ten days, so their kids figure they will have plenty of time to clean up after their party. But what they haven't anticipated is that everyone from school and all their former classmates know of the party.

The party begins to take shape around 6:00 p.m., when the circle of friends shows up. Jake and his sister Jan are there. Jan is best friends with Dawne and Judy. Judy came to the party with Pamela, Jake's girlfriend. Marie and her brother Schibe are there, along with sisters Terri and Tina Jones. Greg Parrish, one of Jake's two best friends, completes the early crowd.

The party begins very upscale, as Dawne and the girls prepared for this party much as their parents would. There are plates and bowls of munchies on every table in all the common rooms. The kitchen area is where many of the girls are congregating, and the back deck, outside the kitchen door, is beverage central. On the right is a steel tub full of sodas and bottles of water. Sitting in Styrofoam tubs are two kegs of beer—a light domestic beer and a local micro-brew favorite.

On the left are two card tables with glasses, napkins, and two glass punch-bowls filled with ice surrounding a dozen bottles of wine. Everyone knows the guests will supply some hard alcohol during the course of the party.

By ten o'clock the streets are full of cars, and the house is wall-to-wall with partying youth. The crowd is fairly well behaved, but Blink, Dawne,

4

and their circle of friends know all too well what can happen at parties like this.

As the party escalates into a loud obnoxious event, the guys hang out in the living room, while the girls stay gathered in the kitchen. Jake notices Rickey Magerro and some of his boys are in attendance, smoking cigarettes at the base of the staircase. Rickey was the toughest bully Jake faced in his childhood. For years Rickey and his thug friends always threatened Jake and his friends, whenever they saw them in the neighborhood.

Jake will never forget how fast his heart raced some years ago, when Rickey grabbed him by the shirt and slugged him in the stomach and the jaw. His jaw hurt for almost three weeks. Jake was scared of Rickey for quite a few years, but in high school, things mellowed out between them, as Jake was popular and an athlete, liked by most. Now, Jake says "Hi" to Rickey when their paths cross.

Rickey and his boys are circling the living room, eating and drinking all they can.

"Hey, Rickey," says Jake when Rickey is within hearing distance.

"What's up, punk?" replies Rickey. "Where is that hot sister of yours?"

"Oh, she's around," responds Jake.

They make small talk for a few minutes. Then, as Jake turns his head to hear what Greg is saying, Rickey slips a powdery "mickey" into Jake's beer. Shortly thereafter, Rickey and his boys move on, while Jake drinks his heavily drugged beverage.

Kevin Gregg, Jake's other best friend, gets to the party late. As he gets to the living room where his friends are gathered, he does not like his best friend's behavior. Sure, everyone is having fun, but Jake is getting out of control in an unbecoming way. He is slurring his words and cussing—very much unlike his usual demeanor.

"What the heck happened to you, Martee?" asks Kevin.

"I'm messed up, my man. The beer is killer," replies Jake. "I'm trying to get the nerve up to fight that stupid bully Rickey Magerro. I'd clean his clock!"

"He'd kill you," Kevin immediately responds, and then quietly asks, "Who invited that scumbag to the party anyway, and when the heck have you ever wanted to fight?"

Then Kevin looks at Greg, jerking his head at Jake, and asks, "What happened to him?"

'I don't know," replies Greg.

Greg turns to Jake and asks, "Did you take some shots of tequila, or some pills, or something?"

"Heck no. I don't do that stuff. Just the smell of tequila makes me feel ill," responds Jake.

Kevin makes his way through the noisy party into the kitchen in search of Jake's girlfriend.

He forces his way to the middle kitchen table where the girls are hanging. He sees Pam and edges toward her. She sees him and acknowledges his presence.

"What happened to Jake?" he asks her.

"What do you mean?" asks Pamela.

"You haven't seen him? He is almost spinning; he is so messed up. Has he been drinking that heavily?" asks Kevin.

"You are joking, right?" says Pam, hesitantly. "What the heck are you talking about? You are such an ass."

"Oh, yeah? Thanks a whole lot. I come to you because our best bud is definitely not himself, and you make fun of me?" Kevin retorts. "Follow me. You have got to see for yourself."

They fight their way out of the kitchen and squeeze past the rows of people lining the hallway to the living room. Finally, they get to Jake and the guys. Jake is listless, staring at the table in front of him.

"Jake!" yells Pamela. She repeats his name, louder this time.

Jake looks up at Pamela and smiles. "Hi, beautiful! You are such a wench."

Pam looks at Kevin, who shrugs. "Oh my God!" Pam says. "You have got to help me get him out of here. Maybe we can hide him upstairs, or somewhere where he will sober up."

"No, I know what to do," says Kevin. "Help me get him to my car. No one is home at his house, so I'll take him home and he'll be fine. Trust me, his folks are with mine at the dance club. Tonight kicks off their season."

"Good idea. I forgot about the dance club. It sounds kind of fun. I'll tell Jan about Jake after you take off," says Pam. "Help us, Greg."

The two guys grab him by the arms, "Come on, Jake buddy," says Greg as Kevin and he help Jake to his feet.

Kevin and Greg have little difficulty getting Jake to the car, with Pam tagging along. Jake does not want to leave, but his is no shape to argue or rebel. He wants to lie down and close his eyes.

"Thanks a million, you guys," says Pamela. "Take good care of my Jake!"

"You got it," says Greg as the two of them load Jake into Kevin's car.

Kevin helps Jake through the front door of his house and guides him to the couch in the living room. "Let's get you up to bed," says Kevin.

Jake barely musters enough energy to get upstairs with his friend's assistance. He falls on his bed, Kevin helps him off with his shoes, and he immediately passes out. Kevin pushes him all the way onto the bed, throws a blanket over him, and locks the doors on the way out of the house.

Jake awakes in his dream with his head spinning painfully. The mixture of the different types of alcohol, combined with the strength of the mickey, is synergistically strong.

Jake starts having hot, sweaty, painful hallucinations. He finds himself dry-throated and thirsty, lost on a dirt road baking under a sweltering sun. A large black dog grabs him by the ankle and hurts him badly. He kicks strongly to get the dog off his ankle, and the dog releases his foot and latches on to his stomach. The pain is excruciating. Jake pulls the dog away as he leaves the dry road of his dream for skies black with terror. Around him now is nothing but darkness and gray, cliff-like backgrounds. He feels as if he is losing his energy and his way, and starts shivering. The pain in his stomach worsens, and he finds himself falling away from the gray cliffs. He sees a flailing metal ladder-like staircase, hanging precariously off the gray cliffs, descending into the darkest, deepest pit of gloom below. He barely grabs onto the stairs as they swing by. Although the staircase stops his fall, the rungs are treacherous: first cold, and then hot, and then greasy. Jake fights the stairs for quite some time, feeling that if he lets go, he will die.

After what seems like hours, it occurs to Jake that letting go would be simple and easy.

"What would it be like to float off these stairs and glide into the dark?" Jake thinks. "Should I?"

A chorus of voices startles him: "Go ahead, let go. The struggle will be over and you will be safe from the stairway forever."

He sees weird streaks of black puffs, which look like both animal and human faces.

"Go ahead, quickly, let go!" he hears.

"No!" Jake conveys to himself.

He grabs the staircase as tight as he can. He wraps both arms completely around the ladder and himself.

"I won't let go!" he yells out.

Once again, scenes of his life flash in front of him.

Pamela and he are at their favorite getaway, parked along the lake, watching the waterfowl and breathing fresh air.

"This is my favorite place in the world," Jake gently says to Pam. "I could sit here with you and watch the birds and the world go by forever." They look at each other and smile. Suddenly, a heavy gust of wind and dirt blows into their faces.

Now he sees mom and dad kneeling in church, praying to God to give them a reason their Jake was taken from them at such a young age.

"Mom! I am right here! Over here! Can't you see me, Mother? Mom!" pleads Jake.

Mom drifts off into the nothingness as Jake clings to the staircase. He now sees scenes of war on a distant hill—now near, now far.

"So many lives lost at war," Jake thinks. "Why do so many people have to die needlessly?"

Sadness wells up in him. "Why is this happening to me? Is this it? This is all that is in store for me?" he thinks.

But Jake continues to hold on tightly. Voices and intense, vile laughter resonate in Jake's eardrums. He is fighting the most intense battle versus the devil.

He wants to help himself, but he feels as if time is running out. The voices and laughter seem as if they are going to crush his ears and his head. The stairway is getting hotter and greasier, making it very difficult to continue to hang on.

He thinks of giving up, when he finds himself on the football field, sweating profusely. "Don't let go. Push yourself. Make it hurt!" screams Coach Ryan.

Back on the staircase, the brightness is diminishing while the vile laughter intensifies. The cold darkness yearns for Jake's presence as his heart is being pushed to its physical limits. Looking up the cliff, he sees that the staircase is hanging by a thread. Jake feels his breath losing its strength. The situation appears to be coming to a close. Jake can now see the bottom rungs of the staircase, each one covered with maggots.

"*No!*" screams Jake, "This cannot be happening to me. I believe in good. Why me? *Please! Please! Please! Help me! Somebody, anybody, please help me!*"

Jake puts his thoughts in front of all the noises, voices, and smell. He concentrates hard on good things.

"People die too early all the time. Why should I be different? Because I am different!" Jake tells himself.

Then Jake remembers his tenth birthday party and the same feeling of approaching the darkness of evil.

"The experience, the smiling cloud," he thinks. "*Yes, that's it!*" he shouts aloud. "*You! Yes, you! Where are you?*"

In an instant, his heart and soul are enveloped by the most warming, fulfilling feeling any human could ever enjoy. Suddenly, the atmosphere is filled with distant clouds—fluffy banks of bright clouds, with different shapes and colors. As the massive banks of goodness drift closer to Jake, he can see the smiling face growing clearer by the second. The peaceful, loving figure exudes comfort. Jake is not spoken to, and he does not speak. He feels himself looking at the figure, and he looks at Jake.

The clouds drop Jake safely in a familiar part of his sleep, in the confines of his own room. For the second time, our Creator has saved Jake from the devil's drastic reach.

———

In the morning, breakfast—indeed, life itself—has a special savor for Jake. He remembers his dream, shivering at the thought of the frightening staircase. Little does he know he had been drugged, but if he did, he would not care, because he is so grateful to be alive.

"Today is different," he tells himself. Something good is happening, and Jake can feel it deep inside.

Of this excitement, Jake gives no outward sign, because he has cultivated the ability to hide his enthusiasm at the right time. This is because his friends and family tease him about being hopelessly optimistic. Privately, Jake knows his optimism to be much healthier than the pessimistic attitude that occupies too many humans today.

But Jake keeps his night's dream and his morning's insight to himself. After breakfast, Jake helps Mom clean the kitchen. He organizes his room a bit, and then calls Kevin. They do not have to work at their summer job at the paintbrush factory today, so they are going to work out and then go to the mall with the girls.

The day goes well for Jake, and he finds himself really getting into life around him. The fresh air, the clouds in the sky, the smell and colors of every flower and bush they pass—all fascinate Jake.

Everyone they see who was at the party is happy to see Jake, and they ask him how he is feeling. He answers all the questions as well as he can, and is relieved when the questions cease.

After the mall, they go their separate ways. Jake has some catching up to do at the library. Afterward, he stops at the grocery to pick up some brown rice for his mother.

That night, the entire family is together for a baked chicken meal Mom has prepared. Everyone is curious as Jan answers questions about last night's party. Jake really only knows what he heard at the mall.

"What happened to you last night, little brother?" Jan asks Jake.

"I was not myself, that's for sure," replies Jake. "I do not remember much of the party after all the people showed up. To top it off, I had the strangest nightmares."

"Who is this kid, Magerro?" asks Dad.

"His dad runs the egg plant up Dairy Creek Road. I am not sure what his mom does. His older brother Steve played offensive guard for the Hawkeyes ten years ago," replies Jake.

"What about the party? Did the cops show?" Dad asks Jan.

"The cops arrived about midnight. I thought they would show at ten-thirty. They told everyone to split and not to drive if they had been drinking. I haven't heard of anyone getting into trouble, but it's still too early after the party to tell," elaborates Jan, turning to Jake. "I'll bet Rickey did that to you. He is such an A-hole."

"Tell us about your nightmares, Jake," Dad adds.

Jake begins, "I was really scared. I was hanging on a staircase over a black, deep, bottomless pit. I saw all of you missing me, and I screamed at you, but you couldn't hear me. Somehow, someway, I was saved by a smiling cloud-like figure. It was so surreal."

"Wow, Jake! It sounds like you were drugged. Are you feeling OK today? Maybe you should go see Doc Drake," responds dad.

"I really sweated hard during the dream, plus we worked out after school. I feel pretty good today," replies Jake.

Jake is too embarrassed to tell the family he peed his bed during the ordeal.

"I feel best because I didn't fall off that staircase. It scared the heck out of me," he divulges.

"Mother, did you hear all of this?" asks Dad.

"I'm sorry dear, I was on the phone. What happened to Doc Drake?" she asks.

"Mom!" they all cry.

Dad tells Mom the story as he heard it. She is quite upset. They talk about pressing charges, but Mom calms the situation down.

"You cannot go to the police without any hard evidence and expect anything to come from it. We must be careful," she says. "Nowadays, people like Rickey will sue for slander. Is it worth it? It is much too fine a line and will probably be way too difficult to prove. Jake is OK, and that is the main thing."

"I agree with you, Mom. It isn't worth it," says Jake.

Jake is so glad to lie down on his bed after a long day. He prays with his usual optimism. Lying down on his bed is the best feeling. Sleep is soon to follow.

———

Benjamin Franklin and all of purgatory understand the situation. The second showing of our Creator to Jake has penetrated the intangible barrier between man and purgatory. Now, there is the distinct potential of a living human being participating from within purgatory to help influence the Limbic Highway of man.

It is up to Ben, and all of purgatory, to teach Jake all about the Limbic System. Their goal is to have Jake utilize the methods and reasons of the Limbic System, to assist humanity as never before.

Jake's chances for helping humanity are not without risk, simply due to the daily trials and tribulations of life and the perils of being alive. There are many acts, intentional or random, that lie in our paths and affect our lives, but everyone within purgatory will watch out for Jake any way they can.

Envision man's life as a brand-new spool turning on a rod. At life's onset, the spool turns perfectly cleanly, with no wasted motion or friction of any parts. Egotism, vanity, violence, or any unfriendly human action will make the spool budge or shake, or will do something else to vary it from perfect rotation. Man's Limbic Highway is much like his own spool of life.

Halfway through the night, Jakes dreams he is on the roof of the house. The dream is as realistic as his nightmare last night. He stands at the apex, enjoying the bright star-laden sky without fear, when a magic-carpet-like platform pulls up next to him. It is piloted by what appears to be a man. The man is composed of a neon blue outline with a light blue translucent face and body. When Jake gets a glimpse through his see-through exterior, there is nothing inside. There are no feet and the man appears to hover on the magic-carpet-like platform. He does have facial features and looks like he did when he was alive.

"Hello, Jake!" the pilot says. "I am Oswaldo, from Quito, Ecuador, and you are coming with me on a journey into space. I shall be your tour guide to purgatory."

"Wow! Are you serious? You have got to be kidding. Purgatory? Really?" asks Jake in amazement.

"Yes, my friend—we are truly on the way to purgatory and all that goes with it. Please do not worry; just relax and enjoy the sights."

"Have I died and gone to heaven? Are we safe on this thing?" asks Jake.

"Yes my friend, we are very safe, and no, you have not died but you are going to visit heaven, so to speak," answers Oswaldo.

Jake gets on the platform and they whoosh away, moving swiftly through the earth's atmosphere into outer space. They travel through countless bright, vast galaxies, stars and planets, infiltrated with streaks of stardust and gases and countless patterns of light. Occasionally they pass through darkened space corridors, sporadically filled with deep-colored neonlike designs. On and on they journey, until they arrive at the entrance of the most vivid, celestially enhanced neighborhood imaginable. Jakes feels safe the whole way, but the entrance into the fresh new world, inundates his senses.

The entrance into purgatory is composed of hundreds of massive golden arches, which look opaque. But as they go past the arches, Jake sees they are composed of inner gyrating spectacular golden mechanisms, which produce the false solid appearance.

"This is awesome, Oswaldo!" says Jake.

Once through the magnificent gates, Jake sees transparent, neon-bordered, communities and buildings, stretching everywhere, above and below him. The platform finds its way to a large-scale lobby area, where hundreds of people are waiting for them. Oswaldo stops the platform on the lobby floor. They step off to meet the contingent.

"Welcome to purgatory, Jake!" the crowd hollers.

There are many faces Jake recognizes, and many he does not. By the time the greeting is over, Jake has had short conversations not only with the souls of his family tree but also with many people he admired in life, such as Theodore Roosevelt, John Wayne and Martha Washington.

The last figure to greet Jake is Benjamin Franklin.

"Hello, Jake. I am Benjamin Franklin. Welcome to the intangible aspect of the world in which you live." Ben is composed of many shades of neon blue. He wears dark blue spectacles and his attire is of the 1700s. His voice crisp, clear and resonate. Comforting.

Jake is a bit star-struck. "Hello, Mr. Franklin," he says, awkwardly. "I am so very pleased and excited to meet your acquaintance. I am nearly speechless. You are one of my heroes. I cannot tell you how much we all appreciate what you did for our country!"

"Why, thank you, young man," Ben humbly replies. "Please, call me Ben. You and I have a lot to do together."

Ben explains to Jake, "You have just been on a journey traveling on the Limbic Highway from your house to purgatory, located in the middle of the universe. The soul of every human being on earth goes to purgatory when they pass away, unless they go to hell.

"Purgatory is part of the Limbic System of man," Ben continues. "The Limbic System is composed of heaven, cerebra, purgatory, space as man knows it, the earth's atmosphere, all of earth itself, every human being, and every human's Limbic Highway. The Limbic Highway is the elaborate world designed to help man survive and exist on earth. Not since Jesus Christ walked the earth, some two thousand years ago, has a live human being visited purgatory."

Ben looks at Jake over bifocals and continues, "Every person on earth has their own guardian angel, who is connected to their brain via their own Limbic Highway. I had my own, and you have got yours. The guardian angel resides in purgatory in the live G-A hall region, which is high above us. The guardian angel's residence in the live G-A hall, is called the virmory. The virmory is best described as a computer room, where the statistics of the human being's brain and body are displayed on translucent screens on a console within the virmory's walls and ceiling. The connection of your brain to your virmory is the Limbic Highway. It will make better sense to you after we visit one or more Limbic Highways.

"The best way to learn the system is to jump right in and experience the operation. Before we do, I will set the table, so to speak. Do not you just love language? I tell you, Noah Webster is such a blessing. You will have to meet him someday."

Jake remembers Webster from his high school history class. Kevin did a report on the English language. Webster was a prominent figure in developing the English language, as Americans know it today.

Ben goes on, "We are standing in the lobby of purgatory, and as you can see, our world expands in all directions. The lower quarter, with the different shades of neon green borders, is the administration area. High above the green walls, barely visible from here, you can see the green turn to orange-brown. That is the live G-A hall.

"The administrative section is an elaborate filing system. Almost every dream and memory of every person is stored in this section. When people pass away, their life is scrutinized by the administrative area. The results determine their placement in purgatory," explains Ben. "Many souls begin as a Guardian Angel, or assist the Guardian Angel of a person with similar traits."

Ben takes a second to let Jake gather his thoughts.

"There are many souls however, who are not suitable to hold G-A responsibilities. They are not so bad they go to Hell, but they are not exemplary enough to be a responsible Guardian Angel. These souls are assigned to a different area of the Limbic System, to help fight evil off human Highways," says Ben. "They often become soldiers on an M-C-U, which stands for a Mobile Cleansing Unit—a mobile battleship so to speak."

A large platform appears. Ben and Jake glide onto the vehicle, which is equipped with an elaborate console for Ben to operate.

Their platform rises from the lobby, gracefully floating upward. The immenseness of the administration sections seems to go on and on, expanding everywhere. Eventually, the green silhouettes change to orange-brown colors, and the platform gracefully stops.

"This is the beginning of the Live G-A Hall, says Ben. "All live humans are connected to their Guardian Angel in this section. The sections are coordinated geographically, situated for simplifying communication conduits. As you will see, the Fathers and Leaders of these regions are situated in the same manner. This principle is kept throughout the whole system from here to earth. The simpler the function, the better the maintenance. The less confusion there is, the cleaner the Highway. Before we go into a Virmory, let us take a brief look at the upper two levels of purgatory."

The platform picks up speed as it ascends further into the neon world. The orange-brown of the live G-A hall turns to different shades of blue. The office-like design of the live G-A hall has changed to a rural setting. Buildings shaped like castles and barns are grouped on the landscape.

"Here we are, Jake. This is my home—the home of the Fathers and Leaders. We have exhibited leadership qualities and strong decision making during our lives on earth. We are utilized in purgatory for many reasons. We offer hands-on daily advice and direction for G-As and the purgatorial community. The Fathers' opinion is weighted when the community makes important decisions. Our main objective, though, is to help anticipate the cunningness and deceit of evil," elaborates Ben. "We will observe our section in action later, but first, we need to head upward for a bit."

As the platform ascends, the blue-bordered tiers gradually turn to bright reds, and Jake feels like he is part of the paintings in the Sistine Chapel. The sights and feelings of love are beyond description.

"This is Cerebra," announces Ben.

They are on the border from the Fathers and Leaders section to Cerebra.

"This is remarkable!" gasps Jake. "Are we in Heaven?"

"No Jake, this is not heaven, but part of Cerebra does interchange with heaven. Let me explain. Cerebra is many things. It is the bridge from purgatory into mortal heaven. It is the section where all souls eventually get to visit, if only to experience the feeling of heaven. But, most importantly, Cerebra houses the 'dream machine' of life. Every section throughout Purgatory inputs daily information into the administrative system. The information is utilized as deemed necessary through the network of Cerebra, and the dream machine prompts a dream for the human." Ben takes a break and looks at Jake over the top of his glasses. "Unfortunately, the percentage of dreams that are remembered or utilized is quite meager. But, every little bit helps.

"We are going to see a dream machine in Cerebra and then head back to the Live G-A Hall and visit your Virmory. After that, we'll take a ride on your Limbic Highway. So far, so good, Jake?" asks Ben.

"So far, so good, Ben," replies Jake. "I'm hanging on."

Their platform heads into the middle of the bright red world above them. The sights are brilliant, almost overwhelming, and Jake stares in astonishment with his jaw hanging open. They stop in the in the middle of the largest ballroom imaginable, illuminated by vivid, elaborate chandeliers and enormous, lustrous corsages of lights. In the center of it all is a gigantic stack of virtual consoles, equipped with all the virtual gadgets, monitors, and controls a human could imagine.

"Jake, this is a dream machine, says Ben, pointing at the enormous object. "In fact, this particular machine is the hub of all the dream machines in purgatory."

"The machine processes the necessary information before dreams are produced. The tedious process the administrative section goes through offers Cerebra an instantaneous, broad view of a person's life, utilized to create impacting dreams. Let me put it this way: All the organizing and research done by the administrative and a G-A is saved, and when Cerebra needs information about a human's life, past or present, it is readily available to read in Cerebra. You will not believe how much time it saves in space," states Ben.

"We will see much more of glorious Cerebra later, young man. For now, let us travel to your very own virmory," states Ben.

"Cerebra is way awesome, Ben," announce Jake. "I feel like I am in love with everyone everywhere."

"I know Jake. Cerebra is pure love," replies Ben.

The platform drops like a falling leaf through the blueness of the leaders and fathers section, and levels in the midst of the live G-A hall. They scoot in and out of corridors and come to rest at the doorway of one of the many offices. Waiting for them at the door is a woman, and inside the office, is the coolest chair imaginable, surrounded by large screens and a console ten times the size of Ben's. The woman beckons Ben and Jake as they enter the virtual room.

"Jake, this is Allyson, your guardian angel, and this," Ben indicates the entire room, "is your Virmory."

"Hello, Allyson," says Jake, looking at her in awe.

Whereas Ben is dressed in the 1770s look, Allyson is wearing a modern t-shirt-long pants look, with a bright pink silhouette. There are two neon orange flowers design on her shirt.

"Hello, Jake," she replies. "I am so pleased to meet you."

"The feeling is mutual, Allyson," answers Jake as he tries to get accustomed to the virmory. "Never in a million years would I think I would meet my guardian angel. Unbelievable!"

The entire room is virtualized. The front wall has four large screens separated down the middle, vertically and horizontally, by a deep red, semitransparent partition. Below the four-screen segment is a large console with monitors and switches and keyboards.

"Wow! I cannot believe it! How can a room be so small on the outside, and have this intense, vast world inside?" inquires the awestruck Jake.

"You will never cease to be amazed, believe me," Allyson tells Jake.

Ben can tell Allyson and Jake have hit it off immediately. He thinks of close friendships and smiles.

Ben takes the floor. "Before Allyson instructs you about the functions of the four video screens, let me tell you what is going on with the deep red cross-like divider.

"All the images, pictures and scenes you observe are transmitted from your limbic highway, to your virmory. The reddish trunk partition and all its branches is the thalamus of man. The thalamus is the 'control center' of the individual's limbic highway. All the data entering the brain will utilize the thalamus as a bridge to its destination. Information passes through the limbic/cerebral cortex when it first enters the brain. From there it goes into the thalamus where it measures strength, clarity, and depth of resonance, and then bridges to the bellum where the correct amount of energy is established and confirmed. Then, the information goes back through the thalamus and off to its intended destination," explains Ben.

"The tryphus, which we will explain shortly, surrounds the entire thalamus within the limbic highway, and accesses information about truth, whenever deemed necessary. The tryphus is known as the 'truth meter.' I mentioned the limbic highway is the connection from Allyson to your brain on earth. The limbic highway is best described as a five stranded, heavy-duty cable. The thalamus, considered the main strand of the five cables, is invulnerable. The other four cables are vulnerable to evil attack. We refer to the four vulnerable cables as the 'cable-four.' The screens up front show the cable-four," explains Ben. "The two screens on top are cognizant cables, meaning they pertain to the parts of man's brain where he uses free will, makes choices, and houses his emotions. The one on the left is the Basal-G. On the right is the prio-frontal-lobe, the P-F-L as we call it. The two cables on the bottom are autonomic, meaning they pertain to the automatic sections of the brain, which are not influenced by thought or emotion. They are the bellum and the hypo-bulbo. Automatic responses like breathing, healing, and metabolism are coordinated in these areas, and the consistency of the brain matter is very dense and compact—not very soft and edible for evil barbs.

"The two cognizant cables, the Basal-G and the P-F-L, are more susceptible to evil attack than the two autonomic cables because they contain massive amounts of consumable neural mass, which are the basis of man's free will, thought and decision making. Additionally, less than righteous actions and thoughts allow for leniency in the cognizant lobes of the limbic highway, which makes it vulnerable to dangerous evil occupation. Malevolent habits force the limbic security system, the L-S-S as we call it, to remove the evil, often leaving voids in the substance of the highway. Subsequently, evil barbs often hide among the remnants and pester the system.

"When that happens, the results mount and continue daily." Ben hesitates, and then continues, "The barbs find the cognizant cables softer, easier to devour and penetrate, than the autonomic cables. The bottom line, for evil, is achieving their ultimate goal of reaching the deepest fissures of the brain, which almost certainly results in untimely human death."

"How do we keep the barbs out?" asks Jake.

"Unfortunately, Jake, we can't keep them entirely out of our system. Evil will always be lingering in earth's atmosphere, attempting entry into the brain. The beauty of the whole universe, lies within the power of the L-S-S to keep the evil from amassing strength in numbers and in cerebra's dream machine, which keeps man positive," reveals Ben.

"Now," he says, "it is time for Allyson to explain your virmory. The limbic security system will show itself during her explanations."

"Thank you, Mr. Franklin," responds Allyson.

She begins, "The virmory is a mirror of the workings of man's brain. The guardian angel—the G-A, as we are called—lives in his human's virmory. The G-A has a view of his human's brain on the board in front of us. Look at your cable-four, Jake. The lighting in all four screens is consistent—no heavy flickering or obvious outages."

Jake is looking at the screens of his brain in awe, as each screen is a rolling, gyrating reader-board of his mind. The cables of the cable-four are all different, but viewable at the same time, while the dominance of the reddish thalamus, in between the screens, pulsates power.

Allyson enlarges a section of the P-F-L, enabling them to see neural clumps and communities up close.

"Man is composed of billions of neurons, which, in one way or another, are all interconnected," she says. "Neurons are connected to each other by synapses and conglomerate as neural clumps, pools, and communities. The conglomerates attach in the brain, and the brain attaches to the G-A via the limbic highway.

Evil barbs try to adhere to the neural pools in the cable-four as soon as the cables are in the oxygen of the atmosphere. The evil barbs nourish themselves, and do their damage by devouring the DNA and everything else inside the neuron. Most of the time, evil is eventually detected and then removed by the L-S-S, but evil barbs have found a way to hide themselves among neural voids and dead pools. They live for the human's entire life if they can get away with it, or the ultimate, they create an 'evil bulge,' which penetrates the deepest fissures of the brain, and wreak fatal havoc. The evil barbs attempt to gather mass and get so humongous, that they force the L-S-S off the limbic highway. This is an 'evil bulge,' and the potential of taking human life is very evident."

"What stops them from getting to the fissures everyday?" asks Jake.

"They would if they could. That's for sure," says Allyson. "But they are stopped by the limbic security system. The L-S-S uses two methods to stop evil.

"The first is the limbic cleansing unit. We call them L-C-Us. The L-C-U is a five-dimensional spinning, gyrating, sucking machine, which sucks evil barbs from the cable-four and expels the remnants into the atmosphere. The L-C-Us are located in the limbic layer of the limbic cerebral cortex. The limbic layer is the outermost layer of the brain. After the information is cleansed by the L-C-U, it goes through the cerebral portion of the limbic/cerebral cortex, where it is measured. The amount of information is so immense that occasionally some of the evil goes undetected and enters the cable-four. This happens more often in a person with a limbic highway that is tainted, or tired. The evil barbs get past the stationary L-C-U in the limbic/cerebral cortex and find a section of cable-four inside the brain to occupy. Once it has found a neural conglomerate to hide in and live, the evil goes about its business of devouring neurons and pestering the human for as long as it can go undetected. Ultimately, it tries to create an evil bulge, so the human perishes.

"Evil barbs that get past the L-C-U and are detected by the G-A or the L-S-S are tracked down and removed by a second line of defense. The L-S-S dispatches a mobile cleansing unit—an M-C-U, as we call it. The M-C-U is the other method of extirpating evil barbs. The M-C-U attacks the scene and sucks evil barbs out of he infected area. The M-C-U, or mobile cleansing unit, is just that—mobile. The cleansing unit of a M-C-U is similar in cleansing operation to an L-C-U, but the main difference is, it is attached to a mobile vehicle," concludes Allyson, pausing for breath.

Ben adds, "The problem is that some people have so many infected areas that evil barbs have found a way to hide their presence and be real pests, sometimes for an entire lifetime. For example, if the evil gets into and destroys some of the P-F-L section, behavioral patterns and mental balance are often affected. In the bellum, a person will lose their energy because of evil barb invasion." Ben looks back at Allyson, "Please continue, my dear."

Allyson goes on, "So, your limbic highway enters the brain and is cleansed by the L-C-U. The evil barbs that get past the L-C-U quickly attack a weaker section of the brain, much as predators attack the weakest part of a herd. But the L-S-S and the G-A monitor the highway for evil presence, and once it is found, the M-C-U goes to the territory and rids it of the evil barbs. It seems so simple to detect and destroy the evil barbs, but the more man lies, steals and ridicules, the more places on the highway evil has to hide and grow. Nowadays, the earth is full of violence and greed, and the limbic highway of man is becoming treacherous to travel. What used to be a somewhat simple task for a G-A is now an arduous one."

Ben takes Jake aside and smiles pleasantly at him. "Jake, my boy, the crazy thing about the world as we know it is that our Creator wishes for peace, good and happiness, but man continues to have war and cannot realistically explain it to himself. There is no absolute reason for war. There is absolute reason to live. Here we are today, Jake, well into the twenty-first century, and there are more people than ever on earth. Are we to believe, even just for an instant, that there is even a remote chance for peace on earth? Yet, yes, that is what the Creator wants. Peace and happiness as a way of life. If the people only knew as you know Jake. We cannot thoroughly explain why you're here, but I know it has something to do with what I just mentioned. It is all good, Jake. Go ahead, Allyson, keep on," says Franklin.

"As Ben mentioned, the thalamus is the red trunk and tracts, and it is invulnerable to evil barbs. It houses very distinct important functions and is termed the 'control center' of the brain. At the bottom of the Thalamus is the top of the spinal cord, which goes into the medulla, which attaches to the pons, which connects to the motrex. These are the motor portions of the body, regulated by the brain. They work in unison with the bellum to control energy distribution. The medulla is the concentrated nerve-ending center, which monitors and keeps billions of connections from tangling. The pons is an elaborate buffering machine, which assists in keeping energy from being too strong, and the motrex is the rechargeable power source of the brain," explains Allyson.

"Above the motor parts is the key area connecting man's life with the Afterlife, the reticular activating system. We know it as the R-A-S. It is essentially the limbic window within man's brain. Sleep and dreams are enabled and visualized in purgatory from the R-A-S, which captures, collects, and contains the human's thoughts and dreams.

"Your G-A—ahem, me—and anyone who needs to, can read and view dreams and memories from the virmory via the R-A-S. And the memory banks in Cerebra are available to the L-S-S. In addition, travel into the limbic highway of a person's brain starts and ends through the R-A-S. The M-C-Us go through the R-A-S to get to the cable-four section of choice. You should know two primary things about the R-A-S. First, the information read in the virmory is retrieved from the R-A-S. Second, it is the hub of traveling on a limbic highway," finishes Allyson. "So far, so good, Jake?"

"Yes, Allyson, my G-A!" replies Jake.

"The top portion of the thalamus is the core of the limbic/cerebral cortex. The thalamus below the limbic/cerebral cortex entwines throughout the brain and finishes where the spinal cord enters the medulla.

"And Jake, the next thing I am about to tell you is, you must simply believe and realize you will understand more as time proceeds. OK?" she asks.

"Sure, Allyson," answers Jake as he looks at Ben inquisitively.

"Your thalamus extends from your brain into the heavens above directly into your virmory. Your thalamus is invulnerable all the way to purgatory," says Allyson. "However, your cable-four is vulnerable where there is sufficient oxygen for the evil barbs to function."

"Mr. Jake, there is evil in the atmosphere trying to get on as many limbic Highways as possible," says Ben. "We know that, and keeping them away is another function of our existence."

"Wow!" muses Jake. "I guess it is pretty straightforward, isn't it? It is incredibly extensive, but understandable. Please, continue."

"Yes, Jake," says Ben. "Totally understandable, my boy."

Allyson continues, "The next step is a tour of each section of the cable-four. This will give you an exact look at what the L-S-S sees when it trolls the limbic highway. However, before we tour the cable-four, Ben is going to give a brief explanation of the tryphus."

"Thanks, Allyson," says Ben. "The tryphus is termed the 'truth meter' of man. It is a transparent tunnel completely surrounding the thalamus, kind of like a napkin ring—like a tunnel with the limbic highway going through it. It scrutinizes any and all information traveling within."

"Information goes through the limbic/cerebral cortex, and passes through the thalamus to the bellum for energy and coordination. Before the information disperses to the pertinent areas of the cable-four, the thalamus scrutinizes the destination one last time. The whole while the tryphus measures the information for strength of truth. Doing this establishes emphasis on the pertinent priorities."

"Not only is the tryphus the 'meter of truth,' but it also aids travel within the dense superhighway of bridges and connections in the endocrine system," continues Ben. "The main function is being the truth extrapolator, and it utilizes intangible methods, which render us helpless in our attempts to track it. Please, take over, Allyson."

"The Amy-G, which is situated in the lower section of the P-F-L, is where 70 percent of hormones are regulated and directed to their pertinent destination within the body. The L-S-S can see much of the activity within the limbic highway, except within the Amy-G. Occasionally a trained eye can see the shimmering of hormones, but the beauty of life and the endocrine system, is that it is basically invisible. However, the L-S-S continues to remove evil occupations within, when detected.

"Besides the Amy-G, the gnostic area is housed in the P-F-L. The gnostic area is termed the 'conscience of man' and is concerned with behavioral patterns and mental balance. A person's language and thinking are scrutinized in the gnostic area, before going to the Basal-G section to be finalized into thought, speech and action. But the Prio-Frontal is the section of brain with the highest square footage of neurons, and the softest, easiest to devour neural communities. Therefore, it is the most highly guarded section of the limbic highway. When the two main sections of the P-F-L, the gnostic area and the Amy-G, are invaded by evil barbs, the results are often mean, dirty and maddening," declares Jake's G-A.

"Whew, there you have it Jake," says Ben. "You have heard a few particulars of the thalamus, the tryphus, the prio-frontal and the Basal-G. Now it is time to venture onto your Limbic Highway and see for yourself."

Suddenly, outside the virmory door, there hovers a boat-like vessel. Its rectangular outline is bordered in bright red neon lights. The rest of the vessel is translucent and occupied by eight figures. The front figure addresses Ben. Ben is dressed somewhat like a wooden war-ship captain from Ben's days, whereas the others are dressed alike in a dull red neon outlined tee-shirt and long pants.

"Hey, there, Mr. Franklin. Are you ready?"

"Hello, Butch. Yes, we are ready," replies Ben. "This is Jake and his G-A, Allyson.

"Hi, Allyson and Jake," say Butch, and the two return the greeting.

Ben continues, "This is Butch, our M-C-U captain, and this is our M-C-U. Butch was a mainstay of the American navy during the War of 1812. He was one of the best navigators of the American and French fleets, and his sharp thinking and quick actions helped secure America's victories. He will be guiding the Red M-C-U during our journey. The other seven figures are working souls, soldiers of the L-S-S. Give us a brief explanation of your M-C-U," Ben says to Butch.

"The mobile cleansing unit operates much like an L-C-U," begins Butch. "It sucks and ejects evil barbs into vacuum corridors, which spew the debris back into the atmosphere or, on occasion, into the waste system of man. The large sharp-angled machine at the back of the vehicle is the cleansing unit. Notice the outlets on the exterior of the boat and the conduit wrapped around the rim. We will put the unit into action later. Anyway, there is one main console, plus a portable consoles for each working soul on board."

"Let's get rolling, Butch," instructs Ben.

The three of them glide onto the M-C-U and almost immediately into Jake's R-A-S. Jake is totally in awe. The Thalamus is as solid as it is nonvulnerable, and

Jake feels like he is right in the middle of the busiest electrical city imaginable. The M-C-U follows a neon red track out of the R-A-S into the entrance of the P-F-L.

Ben asks Butch, "Are there any visible, formidable evil barb conglomerations in the P-F-L right now?"

"No, sir, nothing of which we are aware. However, there is some occupation in the Hypo-Bulbo, which we are scheduled to remove shortly," replies Butch.

"That is a surprise! Can we be at hand for removal?" says Ben.

"Yes, Ben, we will make that happen," answers Butch.

"Good. Please continue," responds Ben.

The bright solid sturdiness of the thalamus turns into a wide river of different shapes and sizes of neural pools, industrial synapses and streams of floating debris. The atmosphere is riddled with purplish colors and patterns as they maneuver up, down, and around countless communities of neural pools, until they see the lights of Jake's highway turning many shades of bright blue.

"We are nearing the Amy-G," alerts Butch.

Ben takes over as they enter. "Look at the spectacular Amy-G. Notice the variation from neural clump to clump. There are so many different hormones, which invariably travel, yet cannot be seen. Their origins in the Amy-G are the only place that we can detect when they are operational. If you stay still and stare at one location long enough, you will see the shimmering of hormones. Yours are dark blue and are very difficult to see, whereas a female's shine a bright pink, quite spectacular when you are lucky enough to see them shimmer. Keep on Butch, we've got a busy schedule to keep."

Soon after they pull away from the fabulous Amy-G, the colorful blues turn into a purplish psychedelic hue.

"We are now entering the gnostic area, the most sensitive area of man's brain and life. The dark purple interior areas are behavioral communities and within them, in the tighter clumps, we find where emotions are tightly wound. If these areas get badly infested, rage and lunacy often develop," explains Ben.

They follow the purplish paths through quite a few neural communities and come to a large area of violet, surrounded by an orange community, extending beyond sight of their vessel.

Ben says, "The violet pools with the orange perimeter are where speech, thoughts, and actions are scrutinized. We'll show you the area in the Basal-G where actual talking takes place a bit later. Take us up close, Butch."

Butch maneuvers the M-C-U into the middle of one of the violet neural pools of speech. They shrink down to the size of the conglomerate and settle in the midst of hundreds of thousands of neurons. Inside the pod of a clump, they see the inner weaving of neurons and synapses, connecting and operating like multiple strings of Christmas lights.

"If you look closely, Jake, you will notice a faint steady spark firing, Ben points out.

For a brief moment, the neurons flicker.

Ben continues, "Believe me, it is happening twenty-four hours a day, but is rarely visible. Your healthy attitude emits a power source so steady, it is almost boring, Jake—but not really. When we get to Rickey Magerro's limbic highway, you will see how refreshing your boring system can be."

The vessel streamlines back to the R-A-S and heads into the blue green of the hypo-bulbo, the coordination area of man's energy.

"The hypo-bulbo and the bellum are the two autonomic cables of the cable-four," continues Ben. "Their neural communities are smaller and clumped together tighter than the cognizant P-F-L and Basal-G. This is because there is no free will involved. Therefore they contain less square footage; thus, less potential for evil barb penetration. The bellum distributes strength of power from the motrex to all areas of the brain and body, whereas the hypo-bulbo coordinates the system to operate in unison. The main functions of the hypo-bulbo are cardiovascular and breathing rhythms, metabolism and fluid regulation, and muscle coordination for sitting, standing, walking, and rigidity. Your hypo-bulbo is darker than the P-F-L area, because autonomic function is steady and much calmer than cognizant."

Their vessel encounters a bit of turbulence as it approaches neural pools with black fumes emanating from within.

"Here it is, Mr. Franklin," announces Butch. "Behind those large orange-green pools."

Ben addresses Jake, "The damage should be only superficial, because it is very difficult for the barbs to penetrate the dense, dullish autonomic cables."

"Hang on!" admonishes Butch.

The vessel swings low and left under healthy pools and lifts up, right in front of a voracious dark, ugly evil occupation. The barbs are chewing and spitting their way through neuron after neuron, and a black, cloudlike substance hovers around the surface of the neural communities. Jake notices the seven workers have already strung their conduits into the heart of the mangling and began sucking the barbs off his Highway. Before long, there is nothing left of the evil barbs but patches of torn, destroyed neural clumps. The M-C-U immediately clears the defective remains out of the way and connects the shredded areas together, making it operable. Then, they tidy the whole section to make it look new. The result, Jake thinks, is like remodeling your home, only making it smaller.

"Good job, Butch. You guys are right on!" says Ben. "Let us move to the Appurvesti."

Jake looks behind at the orange Metabolic section of the hypo-bulbo as the M-C-U heads down a different corridor. They arrive to large colonies of neural pools, whose colors are constantly changing.

"This is the Appurvesti, Jake," says Ben. "It plays a key role in assisting the P-F-L with mental equilibrium. When a human gets angry and loses his temper, the Appurvesti buffers the agitated section of the brain to help keep him or her calm and cool, as best possible. A person who cannot control his or her temper nearly always has dead pools in his Appurvesti. This is the one section of the hypo-bulbo where evil barbs can go deeper into the surface because of the strong affiliation with mental balance and the fact it is attached to the P-F-L."

"Is that why we had to cleanse the hypo-bulbo?" asks Jake.

"That is correct, Jake," replies Ben. "Normally the hypo-bulbo are ignored because they are too dense for evil to pursue, but the section we just cleaned was affiliated with the Appurvesti and became vulnerable when you were upset about something. In fact, the L-S-S had cleaned the area previously, but the cunningness of evil hung out within the dead pools."

"I have dead pools?" asks Jake.

"Yes, my friend, we all have them. They appear after the L-S-S has no other option but to isolate evil barbs within active neural conglomerates. Isolation captures and seals the barbs inside neural pools, and eventually they shrivel because of no food. The dead pools no longer offer continuity to the system, and the surrounding areas become lackluster. The L-S-S can go back to the territory at a later date to repair the empty colonies, but the system finds it is not worth the trouble. We will observe many dead pools when we visit Rickey Magerro's limbic highway. Anyway, the system lives on, but the more dead pools there are on a person's Highway, the more tired and lethargic that person becomes."

They move out of the hypo-bulbo, back through the R-A-S, and into the bellum. The neural pools are more uniform in arrangement, and they are lit up with white, yellow, pink, and blue colors.

Ben elaborates, "This is the bellum. It is the collecting house of information and is brighter than its autonomic partner. Information first goes through the limbic/cerebral cortex and thalamus for cleansing and redirecting. Then, the bellum adds the correct amount of energy and repetition needed to transport it to its destination.

"The first pertinent section of the bellum is the disclosure wing, over there, on the right. The disclosure wing gives the G-A an instantaneous read of the limbic highway. In the virmory, Allyson simply checks the upper right corner of the bellum screen for an accurate physical and mental appraisal. The bellum is closely associated with the motrex, the power source of man. Look at the black and white pools beneath the disclosure wing. That is the energy distribution link between the motrex and the bellum. It regenerates during sleep and rest. Most of the motrex is in the thalamus, except this portion connected to the bellum."

Butch moves the M-C-U below the black and white community, leaving the power grids and passing into a community of very large pools, which are colored with pastel shades of brown-green.

"These brown-green pools are the 'damping effect' areas, and they are scattered around the perimeter of the bellum. Power and energy continually flow through man's body, and the damping effect keeps muscles and movement from overextending," explains Ben. "The damping effect is a wonderful piece of work, similar in principle to the mental equilibrium of the Appurvesti."

As the vehicle continues toward the heart of the bellum, the pools take on a pinkish hue.

Ben continues, "We are moving right into the pink-colored surface modulalities section. This section is tied to the sensitivity and nerves of the skin. The skin is an organ with a mind of its own. Here, the specific qualities of sensation determine function. You get pinched or burned, or you flinch, or, you get cold and get goose bumps, and so on. The function and feeling of the skin is essentially monitored here in the bellum."

"Like the hypo-bulbo, the bellum does not get too much barb attack because it is autonomic. The neural pools are much too compact and tough for the evil barbs. However, much like the hypo-bulbo, the bellum will continue to receive random attacks," says Ben.

"What do you think so far?" Ben asks Jake.

"Absolutely fascinating, Ben. It makes sense, and I want to help and be involved in any way I can," he answers.

"Excellent! I knew you would feel this way," says Ben.

"Take us back to Jake's virmory, Butch. We need to drop off Allyson and go see Rickey Magerro's limbic highway," instructs Ben.

Butch adjusts the console, and the M-C-U heads back through Jake's R-A-S and stops at his virmory. There, Allyson bids them adieu, and the vessel scurries back into the live G-A hall, coming to a stop at Rickey Magerro's virmory. They are greeted at the door by Rickey's G-A.

"Hello, Ken," says Ben. "This is Jake."

"Hello, Jake," says Ken.

"Hi, Ken," replies Jake, somewhat overcome by knowing this is Rickey's virmory.

"Our first stop will be Rickey's Basal-G," says Ben as he turns toward Ken. "We will be back shortly."

The vessel heads into Rickey's R-A-S and veers off the thalamus into Rickey's Basal-G.

"Why didn't Ken come with us?" asks Jake.

"Because, Jake, Rickey's virmory needs constant monitoring, and Ken's experience is invaluable. There is so much evil presence on Rickey's highway that leaving his virmory unattended, even for just a few minutes, could prove costly. It probably will not, but if something did happen and Ken was not there, the results would be devastating. That is OK, that is the way it works," explains Ben.

"I must warn you before we go into Rickey's Basal-G," he adds. "It is going to be a lot darker than any section we have seen thus far. Do not be frightened though. We will not put ourselves in any kind of danger."

It does not take long to reach ill effects in the neural communities of Rickey Magerro's Basal-G. A sullen, eerie ambience quiets all aboard, as the surroundings are dim with an occasional splattering of shimmering neural activity scattered randomly among the colonies. There is debris floating everywhere among many large neural pools, which are somewhat separated from each other.

"We are in Rickey's Basal-G," announces Ben.

The crew remains still as the vessel cruises into what looks like a war zone.

"This is just the start of Rickey's Basal-G. The damage has been present for years. Poor Rickey has not had a whole lot of love in his life," comments Ben. "Notice that Butch has veered us toward the border on the right where the light is stronger. You can actually see the red of Rickey's Thalamus in the background of the lit-up communities in front of you. This is the somaesthetic area, where the senses are housed. You can see by the consistent lighting that Rickey has adequate hearing, sight, smell, taste, and touch, which is expected at this age."

They observe the neural pools, and as they pass through the colony, white and yellow paths of light constantly flash, blink, and shimmer. But when they reach the next community of pools, the atmosphere grows darker.

"We are entering the section where speech is formulated," Ben says. "Notice the proximity to the thalamus, similar to the senses. The thalamus plays an important bridge role in speech.

"Remember the violet pools surrounded by the orange balloon-like community in the P-F-L?" Ben asks Jake. "That is where speech and thoughts are scrutinized, whereas it is here where they originate and finalize. The blue colonies are speech. Down the corridor, the orange pools are thought and action colonies. It goes like this. After formulation here in the somaesthetic area, these functions bridge through the thalamus to the aforementioned sections of the gnostic area, where they are scrutinized. Then, they pass back through the Thalamus, and return to the Basal-G, where the speech, thought, and actions are actuated. This is a very sensitive section for man, because the Tryphus scrutinizes the information for truth. Too many untruths force speech to bounce back from the gnostic area without scrutiny. This happens when a person continually talks without thinking, or is a habitual liar. The information eventually is altogether ignored by the tryphus. Healthy conversation becomes complacent, and productive activity turns dormant. A couch potato who lies is a good example of what happens when a tryphus ignores the speech path."

Butch slows the M-C-U to a halt, and they look at the pollution emanating from colonies around the front right area of the limbic highway. Up front to the right, six or seven green M-C-Us wage a battle against a soiled pool. There are several blackish, shredded pools scattered throughout the battle area.

"What's going on, Ben?" asks Jake.

"A typical Limbic battle Jake. Rickey's speaking ability and what he actually says are in no way compatible. Evil barbs have been hiding and occupying neural pools in Rickey's Basal-G and P-F-L since he was three. You would think that the L-S-S could keep the Highway clean after battling so hard. But, first off, evil barbs hide themselves deeply among dead pools and often go undetected a whole lifetime, especially in undesirables. They scatter themselves so they cannot be removed simultaneously. Second, while the L-S-S is waging war against evil barbs and trying to secure and repair sections, Rickey continues to lie, steal or cuss. These actions are not conducive to healing, which we shall discuss soon," says Ben.

The M-C-U moves out of the speech formulation colony and heads back into the thick of the Basal-G. They continue to see maimed colonies, but they are so commonplace they go almost unnoticed. They arrive at a colored, structured neural community.

"The Basal-G is home to the physical equilibrium function," says Ben.

This is termed the "Physical-4""This function is performed by four stations within this community, to help the body move properly. The bluish section you see on the left is the Subthalamic Area, which aids in walking and other rhythmic motions, like dancing. You do not see too much damage, do you? Over on the other side of the highway is the brownish Putamen. The Putamen is a rock of the limbic highway. It is the foundation of solidity and stability in regards to balance within movement—basically our antigravitational mechanism."

The crew does not see any substantial damage as they cruise past the brownish Putamen into an orange hue.

Ben states, "We are passing the Globus-P section. See how the colonies are tighter with smaller sized clumps. This is where intricate, minute concentration is coordinated, such as delicate finger movements. Again, Rickey is healthy here. Up ahead on the left is the purplish Caudate area. Overall body control motion, both conscious and subconscious, is coordinated here. Rickey's physical equilibrium community is healthy, which is no surprise because of his age."

The Red M-C-U heads out of the caudate and continues further into the Basal-G. They travel into large fields of fairly bright, sporadically flickering communities. As they continue, the colors on both sides and behind them change continually, as they are beginning to be enveloped by yellow shades of neural colonies.

"Jake, we are coming to the last concentrated area of the limbic highway within the Basal-G. It is one of the most impressive, important areas of the limbic system," says Ben.

They find themselves in the midst of thousands of yellowish pool communities. Ugly brown and black patches are scattered throughout. The size of the clumps and pools are inconsistent.

"This is the 'healing generator,'" explains Ben. "As you can see, it is composed of thousands of huge neural pools and communities. Every facet of man's brain and body has a coordinating neural path in the healing generator.

"The healing generator is described as the heart and soul of man. It continually rejuvenates all aspects of he system. All that happens within the limbic highway can be affected by the healing generator; that is the way it is constructed. The problem is, the more evil barbs that people get in their systems, the less the generator is utilized."

"The key to making it work is the key to man's life on earth. It operates on the 'power of the positive.' When a person is down on their luck and they know it, often they will pray and ask for help. This prayer and willing request goes a long way. The healing generator condones positive reinforcement at the pertinent area, and good things happen. The Healing Generator has miraculous healing powers. It *is* the miracle within us. It is the heart and soul of the limbic system and of man," finishes Ben. "Take us in, Butch."

Butch guides the red M-C-U around hundreds of large clumped pools and lifts the vessel right into the middle of a limbic battle. There must be a hundred M-C-Us sucking evil from dozens of large yellowish brown neural pools. Butch finds an area turning black and zooms right into the middle. There, they find six large, expanded green M-C-Us, fully engaged.

The ugliness bothers Jake at first because of the heightened battling, but he feels safe.

Their red M-C-U slips in at the base of the battling community, and spins and curves around and around the lower pools, removing the voracious evil barbs as fast as they can. Jake can see the other six green M-C-Us above while Butch works his magic. In a few minutes, they work their way up to the six green M-C-Us.

Jake asks Ben, "What are they waiting for? Shouldn't they clean and repair?"

Ben replies, "This is a tedious battle, Jake. They are waiting for time to turn the tide in our favor."

"What does that mean?" asks Jake.

"The healing generator needs some type of positive feedback or desire from Rickey. Somewhere along the line, Rickey is going to have to think positive and want some help. If he doesn't, evil will eventually outlast the L-S-S and a section in the highway will fail, allowing a fatal evil bulge to possibly transpire. This could take years, or it could happen in a week. All we can do is try to stimulate optimistic feelings everyday of his life.

"The bottom line is that each human is entitled to only a certain quantity of limbic help. This is because there are only so many M-C-Us in the Universe. If this were not the case, the L-S-S would exhaust its armament without knowing the predicament," explains Ben.

Everywhere Jake looks, there are brown and black patches of gloom. They leave the battle scene and continue through the yellow-brown colonies of the healing generator. Ben looks at Jake with inspired eyes.

"Rickey's healing generator is less than 50 percent. If he does not steady his will and karma, he will probably find himself in jail within a year. Who know with these people nowadays? I only know it is not getting easier," says Ben. "Get us out of here, Butch. Take us back to Rickey's virmory."

The vessel turns and swiftly moves out of the Healing Generator area. They pass the Physical-4, and then glide through the R-A-S, arriving at Rickey's Virmory.

"Thanks, Butch," says Ben. "I am sure we will see you soon."

Butch acknowledges Ben with a slight bow, and turns toward Jake. "See you, Jake."

"Later on, Butch. It was really great to meet you and ride on your cool M-C-U," replies Jake.

"My pleasure, Jake. This M-C-U has your name on it."

Ken greets them from the console as they enter the Virmory.

Ben points to Rickey's screen and observes, "Look at the Basal-G screen, Jake. See how dim it is compared to yours!"

Ben tells Ken, "Run the memory of our recent tour of the healing generator."

Ken adjusts the console and looks up at the screen. The lower bellum screen shrinks as the upper Basal-G screen expands. The movie is identical to what they just witnessed during their trip through Rickey's limbic highway. Ken zooms in, and then zooms out, testing the picture.

"Look how we can view our journey. The virmory has the capabilities of doing this for nearly every single limbic moment. It also can display visual dreams or actual scenes from a person's life," says Ben. "Yes, Jake, I know what you're thinking. The memory of Rickey slugging you in the jaw can be viewed and scrutinized. We need to see it. Is that OK with you?"

Jake feels like he is on the spot. He is excited and scared as if he were at the apex of a Ferris wheel. "Sure, Ben. It is all a part of what is going on, right?" asks Jake.

"Of course it is, Jake," replies Ben.

The screen of the Basal-G adjusts to the right size, and a projection begins.

Jake and Kevin are twelve years old, walking home from playing basketball at the YMCA. They stop at the corner market and buy a 'sudden death' three-flavored milkshake for the walk home. Kevin has chocolate, marshmallow and graham cracker, whereas Jake has root beer, cherry and vanilla. They are twelve blocks from home, when they meet Rickey and two of his friends coming around the corner, directly at them. Jake grows extremely nervous and does not know what to do, while Kevin cusses under his breath a bit.

"Whoa, look what we have here," barks Rickey. "It's the little twerp Martee and his buddy Kev. Too bad your sister isn't here, Martee. I might not think you are a spoiled brat if she was standing next to you. Where is she anyway?"

Jake is not sure what to think or say. Rickey's question takes his mind off the feeling of adrenalin racing through his system. "I don't know where she is Rickey," he replies.

"Maybe you should know, you little punk. Give me your milkshake," demands Rickey abruptly.

Rickey does not give Jake a chance to reply before he knocks the milkshake out of Jake's hand to the ground. Kevin and Jake are petrified and stand there not moving. Rickey grabs Jake by the shirt and slugs him hard in the stomach, bending Jake over and making him gasp for air. As Jake straightens up, Rickey swings his right hand from the side and clips Jake in the jaw. Jake falls to the ground, landing right on top of the spilled milkshake. Kevin is about to start swinging at Rickey, but is restrained by Rickey's two friends. Jake gets ups and backs a few steps away from the frenzy. Kevin wiggles away from the two and moves toward Jake.

"You know Martee, if you want to walk around here in peace, you are going to have to pay me twenty a month. Give me your first payment right now, punk," threatens Rickey.

Jake feels like running away as fast as he can, but since Kevin is there, he stands his ground, feeling sick to his stomach after receiving two violent blows.

"I don't have that kind of money, and if I did, why would I give it to you?" says Jake.

"If you don't, I'll pound you every time I see you," insists Rickey.

Kevin intercedes, "I don't think so, Rickey. There are laws, you know. We know people who can stop you from doing this. You'll see."

"Ooh, I'm real scared, Charlie," sarcastically replies Rickey. "Next time I see you Martee, I expect to be paid."

Jake responds, "Sure Rickey, you got it."

Jake and Kevin walk away fast, constantly looking behind them to see if the enemies are following. At first the thugs stay close behind, but after a shortcut through a neighboring backyard, Jake and Kevin lose sight of the troublesome group.

"What a bugger," says Jake.

"Why didn't you hit him back?" asks Kevin.

"I was too scared. Plus, I probably would have got hit even more. I did not like it at all. Neither one of us need any unforeseen injuries, that is for sure," replies Jake.

"Yeah, I hear you," says Kevin. "I wish my older brother was still in town. You are not going to pay him, are you?"

"No way. I would tell my dad first," answers Jake. "He sure scares me though."

"Stop it right there, Ken," says Ben Franklin. "At this time, let us take a gander at Rickey's Limbic Highway."

Ken pauses the projection, and the four screens of the cable-four expand back to their normal read.

They view the screen of Rickey's bellum as Ken searches the Disclosure Wing for obvious damage. There are dark segments in both the P-F-L and the Basal-G areas of the reader board. No one is surprised. Ken pinpoints the damage to the lower portion of the gnostic area, where there is significant damage located in the emotions communities. Ken adjusts the screen and spots damage in the upper section, proving the healing generator is obviously soft. The color is dull and the elasticity appears rubbery. The viewfinder finds one of the larger burned out areas and moves in. At this time, Ken identifies the locations, and coordinates Rickey's past, from the damage. This creates a scene for everyone to see.

"Today, the same areas in Rickey's Basal-G are surrounded by more darkness than before. This shows that the lack of caring exhibited in Rickey's system has been going on for a long time," states Ben.

Rickey sits at the able with his younger brother Steve. His parents will not quit arguing. He is only ten and really does not care about what they are saying. Rickey's only concern is if he and his brother get to go to the season-ending soccer jamboree. This is the first year he has played, and he not only enjoys the game, but is skilled as well.

"I don't have time to take the kids to a stupid jamboree. It is at least forty-five minutes away and will cost me at least half a day," shouts Rickey's dad to his wife.

"You don't understand, do you?" replies Mrs. Magerro, "I am out of options, and you can't help me?"

Ben explains the situation to Jake. "The boys stayed at day care for nine hours that day as they missed the best soccer jamboree of the year. Rickey never played organized soccer, or any organized sports again. Alice knew deep inside that Rickey had seen nothing but abuse since he was two. Rickey's father would not stop drinking and foolish spending. There have been too many times that Rickey and Steve were unnecessarily left at the day care all day long. Eventually, Alice despised her husband and ended up carrying on for nearly two years with a gardener from a local nursery. The lack of caring has left sections of Rickey's healing generator listless, which, in turn, adversely affects the energy and healing in certain communities in the gnostic area. Rickey has learned to accept not caring about anyone. If he cares, the limbic system will help him. This is Rickey's problem in a nutshell," states Ben. "We can find countless episodes of parental neglect and abuse."

"Keep the pressure on that healing generator, Ken. It would be nice to see some glistening somewhere in there." Ben strokes his chin and looks at Jake. He smiles gently. "It is time to move on."

They say their goodbyes, and Jake and Ben glide onto Ben's platform and descend to the lobby section of purgatory. Ben detects that Jake seems nervous.

"Wow. Ben! That was incredible! I have learned so much about purgatory. Tell me I am not dreaming," insists Jake, somewhat excitedly.

"No, Jake, you are not dreaming the way you understand dreams," answers Ben. "This is really happening. You are the first human being to visit purgatory. However, you will not be able to clearly remember what you've learned until you come back to purgatory. All the information you have learned will be accessible, and you will recognize all of it, but not from earth. The reason is because you cannot let the proverbial 'cat out of the bag.' You will not have vivid memories of purgatory while on earth, but you will have influential, inspirational dreams. Dreams that will inspire you to touch the right people, say the right things, and help leverage mankind above evil presence. Don't get me wrong—you will know something is going on, and you will be very confident in the good things of life. Just hang in there, because in purgatory, we all know you are here for many reasons."

Jake notices Oswaldo pulling up to them on his magic-carpet-like platform.

"One last thing," says Ben. "The degree of difficulty for the L-S-S, is directly proportional to the habits of the person. The system is very straightforward, and if man only knew how precious his time on earth really is, many people would certainly act differently. Do you have any questions Jake? And what do you think of purgatory?"

"Unbelievable," says Jake, exuberantly, as Oswaldo listens. "I knew there is something out there that helps us survive on earth. I just cannot believe that I am now a part of the operation. Sure, I have questions, but at this point, I am not certain what they are."

Ben and Oswaldo stand beaming with celestial smiles.

Oswaldo chimes in, "Yes, sir, Mr. Jake. We are very pleased to have you here in purgatory."

"Hear, hear!" adds Ben.

Jake and Oswaldo jet away from Benjamin Franklin and the Lobby of purgatory. The first visit has been nothing short of spectacular for the young college student, just as it would be for any human being. They cruise through the omnipotent gates of purgatory, and before long, Jake is safely in the confines of his own bedroom, asleep in his own bed.

(2)

Two days later, Jake feels great when he wakes up. He is not sure what he dreamt the last few nights, but he knows he is experiencing something very positive.

"Whatever," he says to himself. "I feel great, like I have been on a reality show or something like that."

He dresses in his work clothes and heads to the kitchen for a breakfast of toast, fruit, juice, cereal, and scrambled eggs. Mom's breakfast routine is predictable and comforting. An arrangement of cantaloupe, bananas, orange slices, and strawberries vividly garnish the table with their colors.

Jake thinks, "Little Jon and Jan do not appreciate how good we have it."

Jon dunks and bobs pieces of banana and strawberry in his cereal, creating war-like scenes of fruity floating enemies.

Jan, as usual, is the last one to the table. She is dressed in a brown, one-piece pants suit for working at the pharmacy. She mainly concentrates on the mirror if front of her face, carefully searching for imperfections.

Dad is already at work. He has breakfast at five and hits the road by twenty after, every morning. The fact he deals with different time zones of the world makes it beneficial for him to be at work early. The entire Martee system operates smoothly. Of course it helps that Mom has not worked a full time job since Jan was born. Dad has wanted it that way since the beginning of parenthood, and they have been fortunate to make it happen.

Jake thinks to himself, "We have been so lucky to have Mom around every day, every year."

After breakfast, the two brothers get in the car and go to pick up Kevin. When they arrive, Kevin is running a few minutes late, so Jake and Jon wait in the car. Jake fiddles with the radio, while Jon stares out the window. There are rain clouds on the horizon, while a gentle sunlight brushes the early morning sky.

This is like the old days, when every morning, Jake picked up Kevin for high school. The two of them have been walking or riding to school together every morning since first grade. Thus, taking Little Jon to school before work is not only fun for both of them, but nostalgic as well. Jake and Kevin have a summer job at the local paintbrush factory. The pay is good, the hours decent, and it keeps them both out of trouble.

"What are you doing after school?" Jake asks Jon.

"Tommy and I are running three miles, and then we will shoot hoops for an hour. Why do you ask?" inquires Jon.

"I want to work out before dinner, and Kevin has something going on. Do you mind if I join you?" asks Jake.

"Heck, no, brother, that would be great," answers Jon. "Meet us at the track at four-thirty. Is that good for you?"

"I'll be there," replies Jake.

Kevin runs from his house and hops in the passenger seat of Jake's SUV. The vehicle pulls out into the street and they begin their route.

"Morning gents!" voices Kevin.

"Hi, Kevy," replies Jon.

Jake laughs and greets Kevin, "What is up K-man?"

They take the standard sixteen-block cruise and eventually arrive at the old high school. The police have their usual spot, as they eat pastry while watching for speeders. The cigarette smokers mill anonymously in the open lot next to the tree-lined perimeter forest, smoke and smell emanating toward the street. The social cliques are scattered about the front lawn of school, as gossip and drab conversation buzz about in the air. It appears as just another day at Lincoln High School. They stop by the library and let Little Jon out of the car, while a low-rider with loud blaring bass speakers rolls by them.

"Bye, guys," says Little Jon as he slams the door and hustles up the sidewalk.

"Later," they reply simultaneously.

Jake continues onward, toward the workplace.

"I am going to work out with Jon and Tommy Chock after work today. You're busy, aren't you?" asks Jake.

"Yeah, I've got a bunch of personal things to complete," replies Kevin, "but I'll try to see you later at the girls softball field."

Kevin and Jake go through their usual routine at work. Five hours of loud saws and sawdust, thirty minutes for lunch, and three hours of packaging and stacking. By day's end, they both look like coconut pastries.

Jake drops Kevin at his house and goes home to change into a workout outfit. By the time he gets to school, Jon and Tommy are already running. Jake stretches at the edge of the track, and when Jon and Tommy run by, Jake joins them.

"Hey, Jake," greets Jon. "You remember Tommy?"

"Of course I do, Jon," answers Jake. "Hi, Tommy."

"Hey, Jake," replies Tommy.

"How's your brother Mark doing?" asks Jake.

"Great. He just got a full ride to play hoop at CU," declares Tommy.

"Excellent—that is great news," says Jake.

Tommy's brother Mark played basketball with Jake in high school and was the team's best point guard. After two years at a junior college, he is now has a scholarship to play Division 1 basketball. Tommy also has a younger sister, Gina, who is in junior high.

Tommy and Jon are running a pretty good pace, and Jake has to work hard to keep up with them. While they run, Jon tells Jake Tommy's mother is going to lose her job at the cannery in two months and he might not be able to play basketball this season, because he might have to work to help his mother pay their bills.

"Are there any alternatives?" Jake asks Tommy.

Jake cannot believe it. How unfair it is to everyone that Tommy might miss this season, mainly because of a deadbeat dad.

Tommy's dad, Wendall, is a carpenter who works for his brother's construction company. Wendall Chock and his wife split up five years ago. He put his marriage in jeopardy by constantly drinking and carrying on after work until late in the evening. Tommy's mother, Sandy, had no choice but to divorce him if she wanted to keep her dignity. After the separation, he stayed around three years, and then left town for good. Apparently, he does not feel his children are important or any part of his responsibility.

After they run six full laps, Jake is panting for breath. "Is there anything we can do to help?" Jake asks Tommy.

Tommy shrugs and says, "Thanks, Jake. We'll be fine."

Jon and Tommy go into the gymnasium, while Jake gets in his car and heads to the softball field.

Kevin Greg, and Jake meet at the field to watch the girls play summer ball before they go home for dinner. They talk the whole time about Tommy's situation.

"Here is what Tommy is up against everyday," says Jake. "When he gets home, there is no one there and the place is cold. His sister will be dropped off from the afternoon sitter about five forty-five, and his mom gets home between seven and eight. Tommy heats the house, cleans the kitchen from the morning, boils potatoes and chops vegetables. When Tommy's little sister Gina gets home, she changes her clothes and plays in her room until dinner is ready. In the meantime, Tommy reads the dinner chalkboard and heats the main course in the microwave. He gets a chance to relax from six thirty to seven, so he always sits at the table and reads the sports page. If Mom is not home by ten after seven, Gina and he eat dinner. Most of the time, Mom does not get home until just before eight because she works overtime. Toss in a day of school and basketball practice, and Tommy has a full, responsible day, every day," ends Jake.

Kevin and Greg are quiet after Jake finishes. They all wish they could somehow help the situation.

On the other hand, Tommy is much too proud to want sympathy or to be patronized. Tommy knows there are thousands of people who are much worse off than his own family. He knows deep inside that when he raises a family, it will be different. He swears to himself that he will love and cherish his children, because that it the right thing.

"How do you know Tommy's routine?" asks Greg.

"Jon and I ran three miles with him this afternoon, and afterward, Little Jon told me his daily schedule. The team really needs him to play. It is not fair," says Jake. "You can't blame him, but you'd think there'd be something that can be done."

When Jake arrives home, he can smell the tuna casserole cooling on the countertop in the kitchen.

"Good timing Jake. You can help set the table," requests his mother.

"I'm on it, Mom," responds Jake. "When is dinner? I'm starved."

"Your father just called. He will be here in less than half an hour. Can you wait?" Mom asks.

"Sure, I can wait. Is Jan here yet?"

"Yes she is, and Little Jon also," says Mom. "Have some cheese and crackers to hold you over until dinner."

"Good idea," replies Jake as he takes a few crackers and pieces of cheese off a plate sitting on the countertop.

After dad shows up, they sit down for dinner. The casserole is cooked perfectly and they all enjoy every bite. For dessert, mom serves pistachio pudding mixed with banana chunks and pieces of vanilla flavored cookies.

Jake is plenty tired when he hit the bed. He prays for Tommy's family and his own, but he falls asleep before he can finish.

The next day is rainy, and as they did the day before, Jake and Kevin drop Little Jon off by the school library, and head to the factory.

"Any ideas on how to help Chock?" asks Kevin, leaning out the window of Jake's car.

"Not really. I sure thought about it though," replies Jake. "I get the feeling that Tommy is going to play for the team this year."

"I hope you're right. We should go to the state playoffs, but we definitely need him on the team," states Kevin as they pull into the parking lot at the paintbrush factory.

The day flies by for the guys. They have a safety meeting halfway through the morning, and before they know it, quitting time has snuck up on them.

The two of them go to the gym for a workout after work, and then, after showering, they both head to their homes.

Jake's mom is not home today because she went south for a birthday party and some shopping at the outlets mall. Jake remembers mom told him about her plans, and that he is going to need to order pizza for the family. Jan and Jon are both in the living room as Jake walks through the door.

Little Jon jumps up and asks, "Did you hear about the smoke bombs in the lunchroom today"

"No. Did you do it?" asks Jake.

"Jake," says a disappointed Little Jon. "I wouldn't do that. They let them off at both ends of the cafeteria and smoked the place out. They were only cherry bombs, but they really stunk."

"Did they catch the smokers?" asks Jake.

"Not yet," answers Little Jon. "But the principal was livid. You should have seen her."

"I'll bet. That is enough to get someone suspended, that's for sure. I remember when Schibe threw a dozen frogs into the women's locker room after PE," says Jake. "His mom and dad had had to plead with the school board for over two hours. Schibe was so lucky to not get the boot. Good thing you had nothing to do with it. Right, Little Jon?"

Little Jon ignored Jake's last statement and kept on talking about a whole lot of things. He talked about the prison ball game during lunch hour, and about the upcoming soccer game this weekend.

"Are you coming to my game Saturday?" Jon asks. "I think Mom is going to ask you to drive me and Tommy."

"I'll be there," replies Jake. "Who are you playing?"

"We're playing the Rebels," answers Jon. "We beat them four to three about a month ago. I scored my only goal in that game. Remember?"

"Sure. It was off a free kick from the left side of the box. Nice goal Jon-Jon," responds Jake.

Jake enjoys watching his little brother play sports. His mother and father attend all the games they can, and since Jake has been home for college break, he goes to as many of Jon's games he is capable to attend.

Little Jon settles down and returns to the television. Jake has put his things away and returns to the living room after washing his hands.

"What kind of pizza shall we order?" he asks Jan and Jon. "We know Mom likes the veggie supreme, so we'll get one of those. We still need one more though."

"Pepperoni," says Jon.

"Are you OK with that Jan?" asks Jake.

"Add olives and mushrooms and I am OK with it," responds Jan as she manicures her fingernails while reading a glamour magazine.

"OK with me," says Little Jon.

Jake calls the pizza parlor and orders the two pies.

In the meantime, Little Jon says he is hungry, so Jake puts out a plate of cheese, crackers, and pickles.

"Here, have a few of these to hold you over until we have dinner," Jake tells Jon.

"Mm, cheese and crackers," replies Jon.

Ten minutes after Jake orders the pizza, Dad calls the house phone.

Jake answers, "Hi, Dad. Where are you?"

"I'm on my way home," answers dad. "Have you ordered the pizza yet?"

"I just ordered it from Pizza Block. Come pick me up, and we can get it together," Jake tells his father.

"That sounds good to me. I'll be there in ten or fifteen minutes," replies Dad.

Jan gets up from the couch and goes into the kitchen to cut up celery and carrot sticks and set the table for dinner. Jon sits on the couch watching TV as Jake waits by the window for his dad.

Dad honks his horn as he pulls into the driveway, so Jake gets ready to walk out the door.

"We'll be right back, kiddos," Jake exclaims.

He jumps in Dad's car and they drive to Pizza Block. Their pizzas are not ready, so they wait in the bar. Jake notices Tommy's dad Wendall is at the opposite end of the bar. Wendall is in the company of two large-breasted blond women. The three of them are drinking and smoking. Jake points out Wendall to his father and tells him the story about Tommy and his family. Jake's dad is not at all happy to hear the news. He stares at Wendall like he wants to have a gunfight.

Wendall cannot help feeling his glare, so he gets up and walks over to where John and Jake are sitting.

"Hi, Jake. Do you remember me?" asks Wendall.

"Sure. You are Mr. Chock. Tommy and Mark's dad," replies Jake.

"That's right. You've got a good memory. This must be your father," says Wendall as he sticks out his hand. "I'm Wendall Chock."

Dad somewhat reluctantly shakes Wendall's hand and replies, "I'm John Martee. Your boys play basketball with my sons. This could be quite a year, don't you think?" John asks pointedly.

"Well, I'm not too into it anymore. You see, I moved to Winston a few years ago and don't get over here too often. I sure hope they have a good year, though," says Wendall, oblivious to his family's troubles.

"What brings you to town?" asks an internally irritated John.

"I'm working on a remodel job at Pearl Condos. It is convenient and good money. They are putting us up for two weeks as part of the deal," says Wendall.

Wendall appears uneasy, and wipes his brow. John's glare is becoming too much to handle.

"Hey, listen, you guys., take it easy, and good luck with your basketball, Jake," says Wendall as he heads back to his chair in between the two women.

Neither John nor Jake says anything. The pizzas are ready, John pays for them, and Jake carries them to the car.

On the way home, Jake tells his dad, "What a loser. He didn't even know his kid might not play this year. Plus, why does he think I'm still playing? Doesn't he know Mark just received a scholarship at CU? My goodness! Plus, I thought you were going to lay into him, Pops. What happened?" asks Jake.

"The time wasn't right," answers Dad. "He has been drinking, and I was going to insult him? I don't think so. Good recipe for trouble, Jake. I work too hard and long to get injured because Wendall is an idiot and a loser. Do you understand?" asks Dad.

"You know I do, Dad, I do understand. I really do. Spite or violence are not worthy means for solution, are they?" asks Jake.

"No, they're not," answers Dad.

They get home, enter the house and find Mom is home. They both wash their hands and sit down to have dinner.

The pizza is great. Two glasses of root beer, a dozen carrot and celery sticks, a few olives, and dinner is done. They all enjoy a dish of vanilla ice cream for dessert and then clean the kitchen. Mom likes the idea of a clean kitchen at all times.

It is only seven-thirty and everyone settles into his or her own evening routine. Little Jon is in the bath, Jan goes over to Judy's house and Jake spends a little over an hour online, before coming into the living room to mingle.

Eventually, it is bedtime. Jake finds his way to his room and the comfort of his own bed.

He lay awake for nearly an hour, thinking of his recent, yet foggy, dreams, thinking of Pamela, but mostly thinking of Tommy Chock. Tonight he especially prays for Tommy and all the kids in the world who are neglected by unworthy parents.

Jake awakes in his dream and finds himself sitting on the top, outer spike of the roof, waiting for the magic-carpet-like platform to arrive and whisk him away to purgatory.

The platform appears. "Hello, Mr. Jake," greets Oswaldo.

"Hello, Oswaldo. How are you?" replies Jake.

"Never felt better. Hop on," instructs Oswaldo.

The platform wastes no time leaving the house and rapidly rises into the universe. Before long, they settle onto the lobby of purgatory, where Ben Franklin awaits them.

"Good day, gents," says Ben. "Do you know you are a Godsend Jake? Your humbleness is most gratifying for all of purgatory."

Jake is not sure what Ben means, but smiles and replies, "Well, thanks Ben. It is great to be back."

Oswaldo bids adieu and exits the scene. The guys glide onto Ben's platform, and in no time they come to rest in the doorway of Tommy Chock's virmory. Tommy's G-A is there to greet them.

"Hello Mr. Franklin and sir Jake. I am Mock, Tommy's G-A," says the G-A.

"Hello, Mock," says Jake.

"Good day, Mock," replies Ben. "Get us started."

"Tommy is a pretty good kid. His disclosure wing is very solid. The P-F-L and gnostic area are every well balanced. His Amy-G is somewhat complacent, but its lethargy is attributed to it being a mechanism to cope with the despondence he faces at home without fatherly support. He does not get too excited, which is good. You can see the thalamus reveals his generator is fully operable. Again, the worries he has been going through compare to the anguish of a single mother. Tommy has the ability to stay calm and not let the things he has no control over get to him. It is a very good attribute," says Mock. "He obviously thinks in a positive manner."

Ben steps into the conversation, "When you ran miles with Jon and Tommy the other day, Tommy listened when you talked. Your mentioning of prayer being uplifting and healing has been influential in his thinking. Tommy has been having strong prayers the last two days. His R-A-S is reciprocating his beliefs. The problem is not Tommy; it is Tommy's dad Wendall. Tommy's limbic highway is sturdy and maintenance-free, whereas Wendall's Limbic Highway is not sturdy. It is sketchy and needs constant maintenance, as he has no inner desire to change. This is where you and I try to influence Wendall. What do you think Jake? Shall we give it a try?"

"I am more than ready," replies Jake.

Ben begins, "First off, Wendall's R-A-S and healing generator have become incapable of allowing Cerebra's influential dreams to be absorbed. Let me explain a few things. Prayer is one way of touching and changing a person's limbic highway. Dreams after prayer often enable the L-S-S to identify and access pertinent, needy areas where damage would otherwise go unnoticed. The G-A scrutinizes the dream, accesses the System, and then cross-references and pinpoints similar situations of the past. The next step is to find historical patterns in the disclosure wing that indicate a time frame when hate was happening. Once specific instances are identified, they are researched for two reasons. The first reason is Cerebra can use the memories to create influential dreams. The second reason is the L-S-S can use the information to precisely locate previously undetected damage and occupation, which is more than likely still occupied. Then, the M-C-U goes in and cleanses and repairs areas in need. With more Limbic Highway operable, the stronger is the chance a Cerebra-generated dream will be successful."

"Not only do Cerebra and purgatory use the memories to make influential dreams, but also the G-A uses the information for daily assistance. Simple things can really help the L-S-S locate and stave off evil advancement," states Ben.

He goes on, "Sleep and dreaming are utilized as tools to influence the behavioral habits of a limbic highway. The better you sleep, the stronger the power of the positive. Simply put, this is a key to life. Positive results are a product of positive thinking and action. The power of the positive is the biggest attribute purgatory has to offer man. The human can capture this spirit and multiply it to no end. 'It always works out' should be our motto. However, the system is not solely dependent upon positive thinking. The L-S-S acts positively and is involved daily in each and every limbic highway. The motivation of the healing generator is not only commonplace in the average human; it is also influential in helping the L-S-S achieve steady results."

"Aw, if only everyone everywhere would understand and believe this to be true, there would not be such a violent presence on earth," states Ben.

He hesitates while looking at Jake. "The idea of using the limbic highway of one man to travel to another limbic highway is new to us. The L-S-S has thus far been able to travel on their human's highway only. The L-S-S is able to access and somewhat influence the thalamus of another person, but has not been able to cleanse the highway or transfer dreams. Now, with your help, the L-S-S is able to reach Tommy's father's limbic highway through Tommy's R-A-S."

An M-C-U outlined in bright red pulls up to Tommy's Virmory. At the helm of the vessel is Butch.

They all greet each other as Ben, Jake, and Mock glide onto the Red M-C-U.

"Why is this one red, whereas the others we saw earlier are green?" asks Jake.

"Go ahead, Butch," says Ben to Butch, "Tell him."

"All of the M-C-Us in the fleet are outlined in green, like the ones we saw the other day," says Butch. "Cerebra created this new, hot-red M-C-U specifically for you, Jake! This M-C-U is designated to travel from one R-A-S to another with your presence and assistance, thus accessing and hopefully influencing the limbic highway for a special reason. It is a unique machine for significant situations."

"That is right Butch, this is Jake's M-C-U," adds Ben. "We will refer to it as the Red M-C-U. There will be no waste of time, as we are going to travel onto Wendall's Limbic Highway, going through Tommy's R-A-S. Wendall's G-A, Percy, has given us coordinates in the Healing Generator where an evil barb "party" is more than likely taking place. Butch will guide us into his Basal-G, and we will locate and remove the evil occupying the particular area of the generator."

Their vessel quickly moves out of Tommy's R-A-S and streams onto Wendall's limbic highway, directly settling in his R-A-S. The transition felt like going through a series of waterfalls without getting wet. As they continue into the Basal-G, Jake looks behind the M-C-U and sees Wendall's R-A-S disappearing. They are immediately surrounded by, walls of colorful yellow and orange neural pools and communities. As they proceed, they encounter numerous large cities of dead pools, which have left brownish hue stains scattered about.

Ben explains to Jake, "We did it. It works! We have cross-entered Wendall's R-A-S going through Tommy's R-A-S. Fantastic!," decrees Ben. "This is one fantastic machine."

"Why cannot we access Wendall's system by going through his virmory?" asks Jake.

"We can Jake, but Wendall's system is complacent, and the areas occupied by evil barbs are hidden from Wendall's L-S-S. In other words, the green M-C-Us are not capable of detecting areas that have previously been hidden from them. However, using the Red M-C-U gives a fresh read and will enable us to detect otherwise undetectable soiled communities."

Ben continues as they travel in and out of several gray, ugly dead pool communities. "This is Wendall's brocal area of speech, which is tender from abuse. There is too much swearing, lying, and vagueness occupying Wendall's thoughts. There has been little, if any, recent positive reinforcement. Look there," Ben points to the right, "Even Wendall's senses are stained from attack. You can tell his L-S-S is constantly busy. He is wearing himself thin."

Butch spots clouds of black smoke emanating from a mustard yellow community up ahead to the left. As the vessel draws closer, Jake sees the infected area is quite large.

"Pull up ahead and idle, Butch," instructs Ben.

The Red M-C-U slows to a halt amid the large neural pools of the healing generator.

"Here we are, Jake," says Ben. "The voraciousness you see is fairly superficial. Deep inside of Wendall's healing generator is where we need to attack. Once we remove the core of the occupation, Cerebra will have a much better chance to work its magic effectively. I must admit, this is getting exciting."

"How long Butch?" asks Ben.

"The cavalry will be here any minute," replies Butch.

Less than a minute passes before a squadron of bright green M-C-Us arrive at the scene.

"You know the plan, Butch," says Ben.

"You got it, Mr. Franklin, responds Butch.

Jake can tell Butch is thoroughly enthusiastic.

Half of the thousand M-C-Us behind Butch cruise past Jake's red vehicle and speed right into the thick of the limbic battle. Butch follows them, but keeps his distance while the others initiate. The hundreds of green M-C-Us behind Butch wait patiently. Up ahead, the first battalion is making a quick work of opening a route for Butch. The evil barbs on the surface are cleaned away like removing an oil slick off the face of water. They are finding plenty of dead spaces, but there is also plenty of sustenance left in Wendall's healing generator.

Fifty or so M-C-Us from behind pull in front of Butch and lead the way past the ongoing limbic battle, straight into the heart of the yellowish clumps. Butch follows, and before long, all the M-C-Us are engaged in evil barb removal.

After a few minutes of intense removal, Ben asks, "We are making good headway, Butch. How much deeper until the root?"

"I don't think it is as deep as we thought Ben," says Butch. "In fact, they are giving us the signal right now."

As they approach the end of the dark battle, Jake sees the M-C-Us already mending the inner lining of Wendall's Healing Generator. The colors inside are surprisingly bright compared to the dull yellow they have witnessed thus far. They have made it to the root of Wendall's Healing Generator.

Butch steers their vessel back through the blackness, and they speed away from the battle. They wind their way through Wendall's Basal-G and go into his R-A-S so they can see Wendall's dream. Ben sends a message to Cerebra, and the dream generated for Wendall begins.

In the halls of Cerebra, the Fathers and Leaders have replayed memories of Wendall's life. They found the time period when Wendall's healing generator lost its spunk. From memories and instances taken from that specific time period, they have created a series of dreams for Wendall Chock.

Ben sets up the dream by explaining the situation to Jake.

"Gloria Yvonne Chock disliked her son's wife Sandra," begins Ben. "The hate was so strong that Sandra did not want to talk with, let alone be around her mother-in-law. For the first four or five years after their marriage, Wendall was constantly told by his mother that he should have done better, as an Asian man, than to marry this lady of Caucasian descent. Gloria was terribly old-country and prejudiced. In Wendall Chock, the Fathers and Leaders, saw a man who was treated like a loser by his mother his entire life.

"The virmory of Gloria is soiled with hate, lies, and deceit. She rarely physically hurts anyone, but, mentally, she is a killer. Poor Wendall could never see how a true loving family should be. As a boy, he was ridiculed and berated by his mother. Wendall's father, Mackey, tried his best to love his son, but he was also abused by his wife, and could not get away with loving Wendall as he wished," finishes Ben.

THREE

Wendall's Dream

Wendall is fifteen years old and is sneaking a piece of cherry pie from his mother's kitchen. He does not hear her as she creeps up behind him.

"Who said you could have a piece of my pie?" spews Wendall's mother.

As Wendall turns to look at her, Gloria slaps him hard across the face, twice.

"Stop it mom. Please!" cries Wendall.

She swings wildly a third time, loses her balance and stumbles a bit. Wendall takes advantage and scurries across the kitchen floor, exiting as fast as he can.

He hides in the barn and hears his mother yelling obscenities from the kitchen door. After a short deliberation, Wendall tosses a blanket and saddle on the old horse at the back of the barn, and rides away from his mother as fast as he can.

He feels alone and so unloved. He has never had the feeling of real motherly love. He can only imagine.

Wendall rides and rides. Nighttime is upon him and rain is falling as he reaches a large grove of tall dark trees. He spots the lights of a cabin down a trail in the grove. Quietly he gets off his horse near the back side of the cabin, stands on a wooden box, and looks inside the house. Wendall is curious and hungry. When he peeks in the window, he sees a family ready to have supper. There are two girls, a mother and father, and a young boy who is wrapped in blankets. The father is standing, moving dishes around the table. Wendall can smell chicken and potatoes. His stomach growls so loud, it startles him. He cannot handle it anymore so he knocks on the front door.

The father opens the door and asks Wendall, "Can I help you, son?"

"My name is Wendall Chock. I have gotten lost while riding my horse, which is tied up out back. Can you give me directions back to town?" he asks.

"George, who is it?" asks the mother from the dining area.

"It is a young gent who needs directions," replies George.

"For goodness' sake dear, bring him in here so he can warm up and have some hot food," demands mother.

Wendall enters, shivering cold.

"Everyone, this is Wendall," introduces George. "I am George Schaeffeur, and this is my wife Abigail. This is my son Charlie, and these are our daughters, Celia and Gayle."

They all greet Wendall and the mother insists he joins them for dinner.

After using the restroom, Wendall sits next to Charlie and enjoys a home-cooked chicken dinner served with potatoes, corn, and greens. Wendall enjoys every bite and can tell the dinner was prepared with loving care.

The kids are very well-mannered during dinner, and there is little conversation, as the knives and forks do most of the talking. Wendall notices all three ladies are dressed conservatively, and the walls are filled with old-fashioned decorations.

He is so hungry and the food is so good. Wendall does his best not to eat like a pig, and, not surprisingly, there are no leftovers when they finish. After a desert of cinnamon-flavored dough sticks, the ladies clear the table and clean the kitchen. Charlie lies by the fire reading while Wendall and George sit on the pillow-covered wooden davenport. They talk awhile about different things, but curiosity finally gets the best of Wendall.

"I hope you don't mind, Mr. Schaeffeur, but what is wrong with young Charlie?" asks Wendall.

"He has leukemia. He has less than two years to live, so say the doctors," replies George. "However, they told us three years ago that he only had six months; now they tell us an additional two years. So, we all remain optimistic about our Charlie."

"Do you think there is anything I can do?" asks Wendall.

"Thank you; that is very nice of you to ask. Do you know any baseball stories? Baseball is Charlie's favorite. We try to play catch at least once a day," says George. "Stay with us tonight, Wendall. You should not go out there in this terrible weather on such a black night. We can put your horse in the barn, and tomorrow you can get a fresh start."

Wendall agrees. He lies next to Charlie on the floor by the fireplace. Charlie has a nice feather mattress to sleep on, while Wendall sleeps on a blanket. They talk for nearly two hours, about baseball and sports, doughnuts and firefighters. Wendall really likes Charlie, because he reminds him of how he wants his family to be. He can tell Charlie's family really loves him. He watches Charlie as he drifts off into a seemingly peaceful sleep. Before long, Wendall does the same.

Wendall changes places in his dream, and finds himself at the local coffee shop on a Saturday morning, with a hangover. He is sitting in a booth next to three gents who are talking about last night's high school basketball game.

"Can you believe last night's game?" asks patron number one. "We had them the whole way. I can't believe those stupid turnovers down the stretch. Tommy Chock would have never thrown it way so many times if he was in the game. What a bunch of rubbish."

"It sure is bogus," says patron number two. "Why on earth would a kid with so much talent want to work during his senior year instead of playing hoops on a top team? I can't figure it out."

"I heard his mother lost her job and he has a deadbeat, lush dad who doesn't care about his family," says the third patron.

"What's that about?" asks patron number one.

"He's a contractor who moved out of town after getting divorced. Word is that he hangs out with loose women, drinks too much, and spends his money lavishly. I guess he's barely paid any child support since he left town years ago," reports patron number three.

"What a bunch of hogwash," spits patron number two.

Wendall cannot believe what he is hearing. "Am I really that guy?" he asks himself.

Trying not to act obvious while listening to his restaurant neighbors, he reads the local newspaper. The first section he turns to is the obituaries. He is shocked by what he sees.

'Charlie Schaeffeur, age twenty-two, died last week from complications during surgery relating to leukemia. Leukemia won the battle, but only after ten years of courageous fighting.'

Tears fall on Wendall's cheeks as he grieves for little Charlie.

The conversation from the booth next to him, and the terrible news of little Charlie, makes Wendall very sad and uncomfortable. He puts his head down on the counter and cries until he sleeps.

FOUR

"Current Time"

Back in his bed at the condo, Wendall wakes up shaking. His head is filled with fresh memories of personal ineptness. The first thought in his brain is that he misses his children, badly. He feels rotten the whole day at work. He pounds the same thumb twice with his hammer and argues with his coworkers over nothing. He has a light dinner after work, and then begins to drink and lament because the pain of last night's dream bothered him all day long.

Wendall wakes up the next morning alone. Again he has a pounding headache and a continuing sense of guilt. After a shower and some coffee, Wendall dresses and readies himself for the day. A resounding knock on the door breaks the early morning condo silence.

Wendall opens the door and is greeted by a cleanly dressed, middle-aged man.

"Good morning. My name is Clyde Glickmere. Are you Wendall Chock?" the man asks.

"Yes I am," replies Wendall. "What do you want?"

Clyde responds, "I work with Acme Collections. I am here to collect any or all of the delinquent child support you owe your family. Do you understand?"

Wendall quickly answers, "Yes, I do. I want to make everything right today. OK? I will go to my ex-wife's house right now. Do you want to go with me?"

Clyde doesn't hesitate. "Absolutely. I am ready when you are."

After a few minutes of getting ready to leave, Wendall calls his coworkers and tells them he is running late because he has an important errand to run. He also apologizes to them for being an idiot yesterday.

Ben is ecstatic. The L-S-S has accomplished an intervention using one family member's R-A-S to access the Limbic Highway of another family member. Ridding Wendall's Healing Generator of the root of a lingering evil community enables the dream Cerebra generates to penetrate Wendall's R-A-S and influence his life. Wendall had shut off the positive flow in the Healing Generator, which, in turn, would not allow his R-A-S to access and comprehend Cerebra's dreams. There was no hope on any near future horizon. Now, thanks to Cerebra's dream getting through, Wendall wakes up to realize he is a real loser and he is ruining his family's life. But he is a loser with a chance of redemption, and he hopes things can only get better with some effort on his part.

Ben addresses Jake, "There are a few things you did not witness that contributed to our success. We knew going in that Wendall's Basal-G was less than pristine. So, while the L-S-S attacked the Healing Generator, we sent twenty-five M-C-Us to the Brocal Area, and they cleansed years of verbal abuse out of the speech community. He should swear less and think more before talking. In addition, your father contributed to the cause. Cerebra alerted him subconsciously of the idea to send the bill collector to Wendall's condo while he is in town. Brilliant move, I must say. Let's watch it go down."

Ben and Jake gather around the large console on Ben's platform. Ben adjusts a few levers, and a movie screen lights up in front of them.

"Honey, wake up. I have a brilliant idea!" Jake's father says to his sleeping wife.

Martha remains still. She is awake, but not ready to engage in conversation.

"Wake up, honey. I've got exciting news," says John.

Martha turns over in bed and finally opens her eyes, looking at John and says, "What is it, honey? Are you late for work again?"

"No dear, nothing like that. I have figured out what I can do to help Little Jon's friend Tommy Chock," elaborates John.

"Oh, really?" questions Martha, showing a bit more interest. "Are we going to adopt him?"

"Funny, Martha. You'll see. Do you want to hear about it?" asks John.

"Can't this wait until later? Please?" asks the slumber-craving Martha.

"Of course it can, dear," says John. He turns off the light and they go back to sleep.

Later that morning at work, John looks at the clock and picks up the phone.

"Fred Johnson?" asks John.

"Yes, this is I," replies Fred Johnson from the other end of the phone.

"This is big John," says John. "How the heck are you?"

"John Martee! Long time no hear. I shot a 78 at the Gull this morning," says Fred.

"Good ole Fred. Always time to play golf. You must have started early," replies John.

"Six a.m. tee-off. I love this time of year," says Fred Johnson. "So, what's up?"

"I want to take you up on that favor you owe me from when I helped out at the kids' wrestling tourney," says John. "You remember, don't you?"

"Of course I remember. What do you need? You name it," he replies.

"Can you send a collection officer to the Pearl Condo this week? We need to serve notice to a deadbeat dad who is in town for a couple of weeks. What do you think?" asks John.

"No problem, Martee. This is easy. Who is this guy?" asks Fred.

"Wendall Chock is his name. His kid Tommy is a friend of Little Jon's, and they play hoop together. He is way overdue with child support, and his kid might have to work after school instead of playing basketball. It is quite ugly," explains John.

"No problem, big John. Give me the details and I'll send someone over there within 48 hours. We must play some handball. I just joined this private club over by Bamboo Mall. They have indoor tennis courts, four racquet courts, indoor golf, and five or six saunas. I can get you in for nothing a bunch of times. What do you think?" asks Fred.

"I'm in. I need the workout, that's for sure," replies John. "Hey, thanks for this. I hope it instills some fire in this idiot's craw."

"You got it Martee. Call me soon for a handball or racquetball game, OK?"

"OK, Fred. Thanks again," says John.

Ben looks at Jake and says, "Your father is all right, Jake. You are very fortunate."

"I know, Ben," Jake replies. "Our entire family is very lucky. So, does this mean Tommy is going to play ball this year?"

"Sure looks that way, doesn't it?" beams Ben. "Our second visit has come to an end, young man. Go now and be well. We will be seeing you again soon, I am sure of this."

Butch takes them out of Wendall's Virmory, and they skirt past the Live G-A Hall and past the Admin section to the Lobby.

Jake sees Oswaldo pulling up next to them, says goodbye to Ben, and glides onto the earthbound platform.

"See you later, Jake," says Ben. "I look forward to our next visit."

"Thanks, Ben. The feeling is mutual. Later!" replies Jake.

Oswaldo and Jake smile and nod their heads at Ben as the platform speeds off through the magnificent gates of purgatory, bound for earth.

(3)

Today is the last day of Jake and Kevin's summer job. Jake will have two full weeks off before he goes back to college for his junior year. Their summer job at the paintbrush factory has been quite a privilege. Not only did they work a good eight to five daytime shift, they also earned a respectable fourteen dollars an hour wage.

During the summer, Dad gave Jake his blessing to move off campus by Thanksgiving break, so Jake has been saving money for a smooth transition. However, the need to save has not deterred him from planning some fun with his friends before heading back to college.

Pamela is only free during Jake's second work-free week, so Jake intends to hang out with Kevin and Greg the first week.

Jake's sister Jan is entering her senior year in college. She and Jake talk every week about the future. She wants to be a pharmacist and has worked the last two summers as an intern at Albert's pharmacy. She is on track to go to graduate school the following year in New York. Jan has always had excellent study habits and guided Jake with his habits throughout all his school years. Jake will always be grateful, and tries to spoil his sister when he can.

Kevin is waiting on the front porch as Jake gets to the Greggs' house at the usual time. It is going to be a very warm day, and Kevin wears only a T-shirt instead of the standard hooded sweatshirt he normally sports over his work-wear.

He gets in the vehicle and complains, "Can you believe how hot it is already? It's only seven forty-five, and it is eighty-eight degrees outside. Plus, the humidity is choking, don't you think?"

Jake replies, "If it is one thing I cannot handle, it's humidity. There is no solution when you're in it, except to get out of it."

They go to work and settle into their usual work routine. Today their fellow workers are making fun of the two of them, because this is their last day of work before going back to school. Jake doesn't mind, because deep down he knows they all wish they had a future in mind other than the paintbrush factory.

He is excited about the next two weeks. He really hopes he can finish off a great summer nicely by really hitting it off with Pamela. He badly wants to make love to her before going back to school, but Jake is shy and finds it difficult to say and do the right things when it comes to love. Regardless, Jake is looking forward to his last two weeks of summer vacation.

After work, he drops Kevin off at his house and heads to the gym for a workout. Kevin would normally go with him, but he has to take his little brother to a doctor appointment thirty miles away.

On the way to the gym, Jake stops at a convenience store for a bottle of water and a chocolate bar. He eats half of the candy bar before he leaves the parking lot. As Jake gets ready to back out, an older-model brown station wagon pulls in next to him on the right. Jan's friend Teri Jones gets out of the passenger side. Jake can see Teri's mother is driving, and her sister Tina is in the back seat behind Mom.

"Hey, Jake!" says Teri as she shuts the door.

"Hi, Teri," replies Jake. "How's your summer going? Are you ready for school?"

"Summer has been OK. I'm not sure about school. You'll have to ask your sister what I mean. I've got to run. See you later, Jake," says Teri as she walks away from the conversation.

Jake is puzzled by her reactions. As he starts the car, Tina rolls down her window and speaks to Jake. "Say hi to your little brother Jon for me."

"Hi, Tina—I sure will," replies Jake.

Jake waves at Mrs. Jones and Tina as he backs out of his parking spot, and then he heads to the gym.

He enthusiastically works out today as he is inspired by the thought of his upcoming two weeks of freedom. Additionally, his recent subliminal dreams continue to fuel his optimism. He constantly finds himself scrutinizing people's lives and thinks everyone should think and act more positively. He is very curious about what he heard in the parking lot of the Quick Mart, and tells himself he must remember to ask Jan what Teri meant when they are at the dinner table.

When Jake gets home, the house smells of turkey and stuffing cooking. Jake goes in the kitchen and sees his mother at the sink, cleaning dishes.

Mom sees Jake walk in and halfheartedly states, "If only cooking didn't produce so many dirty dishes."

"What's the occasion, Mom? Turkey in August?" asks Jake.

Mom replies, "I got a deal on a little tom and could not resist. Plus, we can have turkey sandwiches for two days. I thought you liked turkey?"

"Of course I do. I didn't mean it that way. What I meant is, why do you work so doggone hard everyday?" Jake explains.

"Is it that bad?" mom asks they both laugh.

"Yes, it is *that* bad. How do you expect me to live off campus when I cannot prepare my own meals?" he replies sarcastically.

"You are such a spoiled child my dear. My heart bleeds, only for your stomach," mom returns the rhetoric.

"That's not funny, mom. I will surely miss your cooking, if not you," Jake mockingly replies.

They continue to share a good laugh and prepare for dinner.

Jake worries a bit when he thinks about living on his own. However, the past two years of college has been invaluable experience, and Jake knows that living on his own is definitely what is best for him.

The Martee children have been lucky their whole lives because their mother has not had to work during their childhoods. In fact, she dedicated all those years to her children. She did everything for them, from caring for them when they were sick, to driving them to every imaginable kids' event. She even sewed their costumes from scratch year after year.

Dad arrives home just after six and is greeted at the door, by Little Jon who rushes up and hugs his pop.

"What do you want now son?" asks Dad wholeheartedly.

"Aw, Dad, that's not fair. Aren't you glad to see me?" asks Little Jon.

"I am always happy to see you everyday!" replies Dad.

Mom walks in from the kitchen. Dad walks over to her and gives her a short kiss on the lips.

"How was your day honey?" she asks.

"Great! How was yours?" he responds.

"Just fine, thank you," she replies.

"Something smells awfully good, my dear," says dad.

They all settle down to eat. During dinner, Mom is the first to speak. "Honey, do you know today was Jake's last day of his summer job?" Martha asks her husband.

"Yes dear, Jake and I have been talking. Two weeks of free time is finally here. Now it's time for Jake to come work with me for ten days," says John, deadpan.

Jake looks astonished, *"What?"*

"You know I'm joking, Jake. You deserve a few weeks off. What are you going to do?" asks dad.

"The guys and I are going to play some golf, see some live music somewhere, check out a baseball game or two, and maybe play in a pool tournament next weekend. Pam is off the following week, and we hope to camp out for a few days somewhere. Blink's grandfather's cabin up the mountain might be open two nights. You know the place, Dad. It's fifty-fifty, but ultimately, it depends on if Pam wants to go or not," says Jake. "All I know is it is going to go fast."

They continue to enjoy their meal when Jake remembers seeing Teri at the store.

"Hey, Jan. I saw the Jones girls at the store today. Mrs. Jones, Teri and Tina. By the way, Tina says hi, Jon," Jake says to his little brother. "I asked Teri if she is ready for college and she told me to ask you about it. What gives?

The table is quiet as the family looks at Jan, "Teri is pregnant. Jeremy Brown is the father. This really screws up her plans for college. We all can't believe it."

"Can't she still go to school?" asks Little Jon.

"Not really, little bro. I know she barely made it financially the last three years. Neither of their families is well off enough to be able to pull it off. No way," says Jan.

"Wow!" intervenes Mother. "That family is constantly having this happen. Don't they know what safe sex is?"

"What do you mean by that?" asks Little Jon.

"It means grandparents are often put on the spot when their children, or children's children, randomly have babies out of wedlock," says Mom. "I'll try to explain. First of all, Margie and Harold Jones have been taking care of Melissa's two youngsters for over two years."

"Is Melissa Tina's sister?" asks Jon.

"Yes, Tina and Teri's older sister," says Jan.

Mom continues, "Melissa has been in Las Vegas trying to get her feet on the ground, while her deadbeat ex-husband is nowhere to be found. So, Margie and Harold have no choice but to take care of the toddlers until Melissa can pull her life together. *If* she pulls it together," says mom.

"Therefore, Tina's mom and dad are raising two more kids?" a somewhat bewildered Little Jon asks.

"That's right," replies Mom. "However, it doesn't stop there. In addition, Margie's sister, Chelsea, has a daughter with three kids from three different guys. All three are being raised by Chelsea's father and mother— Teri and Tina's grandparents. They're over sixty years old! Margie is raising two of her grandchildren, and her mother, Wilma, is raising three of her great-grandchildren.

"And I'm not finished," Mom continues. "Margie has two older stepsisters, each of whom has been married more than twice, with kids from each marriage. Their side of the family has so many twists, you need to be a pretzel to keep up with them."

"Wow!" comments Little Jon. "I had no idea. It sounds like a bunch of kids in my school. I always hear about them living with their cousins or stepbrothers, and now I see why. Their parents are not together, or their mothers are not around, or if they have a single parent, they can't afford to live alone. I guess they have no other choice than to move in with their parents or grandparents."

"That is the polite way to look at it, Jon. Would you be happy if I was never around? You might get used to it, but think if your mom or dad didn't live where you live, and you lived with your aunt or grandparents," says Mother. "We are so fortunate."

Mom gets up and goes to the kitchen for dessert. Jake clears the table of used dishes.

Two scoops of ice cream topple the guys' rhubarb pie, while mom and Jan just have one scoop. The conversation continues as they enjoy their dessert.

Dad asks Jan, "What is Teri going to do?"

"She is definitely going to keep it," replies Jan. "Jeremy is going to find a better job, and eventually they want to move in together. For the meantime, she is going to live at home."

"Seems sad wasting the last three years of her college," Dad says.

"True that, but she can always go back to school," says Jan.

"You would think she might have thought a little bit more, before doing what she did," suggests Dad.

"What did she do, dad?" asks Jon.

"She had unprotected sex, and became pregnant," begins Dad. "There is good reason why people get married. They love each other and want to raise a family. Nowadays, so many people don't have the knowledge and the experience to understand that principle. Instead, they act first and think later. There must be hundreds of thousands of unplanned pregnancies a year in our country. These people should use birth control."

Jan speaks up, "You're right, Dad, but I know there is more to it than that with Teri. She has been a good friend of mine for many years, and I really think Teri was not only getting tired of school, but getting scared also. The pressure of all the things that go with school is getting to be too much. She told me that she doesn't think it is worth it anymore because she has struggled for three years financially. Plus, her grades have not been too stellar. Add the fact that her mother has her hands full with her two grandchildren and Tina, and all the circumstances have built up against her staying in school. She thinks it is best to stay here at home and help her mother, who will help her with her newfound condition. The timing isn't all right though—I don't agree with getting pregnant to get out of school. It definitely makes her decision too simple and almost seems like this is happening on purpose. Of course, who really knows what she is thinking? Darn that Teri Jones!" says Jan. "We can only wish her the best, and I really cannot blame her to a certain degree."

The family finishes dessert. Jon and Jake clean the table and load the dishwasher, while mom puts away the leftovers. They all thank Mom for preparing a wonderful dinner.

Jan has left for Dawne's house, while Mom sits in front of the computer in the home office. Jake, Jon, and Dad decide to drive across town and watch the last five or six innings of the local minor league baseball game. The crowds have been real sparse this season, so there should be no trouble getting decent parking and good seats.

When they get to the stadium, they are surprised at the number of cars in the parking lot. They park twenty rows from the entrance and walk to the ticket booth. They buy their tickets and find their chairs, which are located down the third baseline, ten rows up. They are comfortable seats with ample room all around them. A slight breeze cools the warm summer evening. Jake goes to the concession stand and returns with a box of popcorn and a package of Red Vines. Jon shares the Red Vines and thanks his brother. Jake pours some of the corn in a separate box for dad and gives it to him.

"Anyway, as I mentioned earlier," continues Dad, "the Yankees have no chance of winning, no matter how much money they spend. Besides, they lack good starting pitching and tough middle infield defense. Where is the heart?"

"I like the Yankees, Dad," says Little Jon. "Getting that lefty from the Brewers is making a difference."

The guys are enjoying the game when Tina Jones and her boyfriend approach and stand at the end of the aisle, next to Jon.

"Hi, Jon; hi, Jake. Is that your dad?" asks Tina.

Jon replies, "Hi, Tina. This is our dad, John."

"Dad, this is Tina Jones, Teri's sister, and this is Tina's boyfriend, Cat Becker," says Jon.

"Hello Tina," says Mr. Martee. "How is your mother? Tell her hi for us."

Dad looks at Cat and nods hello.

"Thanks Mr. Martee, I will say hello for you," replies Tina. "Are you going out for the school play this fall, Jon?"

"I'm not sure. I haven't thought too much about it," answers Jon. "Are you?"

"I want to if I can talk my mom into it. Let me know, OK?" asks Tina. "Well, see you later. It was nice to meet you, Mr. Martee."

"You too, Tina," responds Mr. Martee, chewing on a mouthful of popcorn.

Tina and Cat turn and walk up the stairs, away from the guys and the playing field.

"You forgot something to drink, Jake," says Dad.

"Oh, yeah," replies Jake as he takes two bottles of water out of the pockets of his windbreaker.

Jake hands a bottle to Dad and puts the other bottle in the arm holder between Jon and himself.

The three of them are enjoying baseball to the fullest.

"Tell me, Jon. I think I have met Tina before, haven't I?" asks Dad, after a while.

"No doubt you have. She and I were born two days apart. Over the years we have attended quite a few of each other's birthday parties, though it has been a few years," replies Jon.

"I remember her from those birthday parties. Tell me, guys, what do you know about Cat? I mean, is Tina going to take the same road as her sisters, or what?"

"Great question, Dad," replies Jake.

"Cat is a pretty cool guy," states Little Jon. "I heard he's called Cat because he was the first kid in his class to have whiskers. He graduated last year and works at the truck barn. Tina says that next year he is going to diesel mechanic school."

"Does she really like that guy?" asks Dad.

"I guess so," says Jon.

"What do you think Jake? I mean, I smell a rat, don't you?" Dad asks.

"What kind of a rat?" asks Jake.

"You know, the kind of rat who will do anything—how do you say—to get in a girl's pants," says dad.

"Oh—you mean, just like any guy?" asks Jake.

"I guess so," says Dad. "It looks like Cat could be one of the lucky ones who actually makes it happen at his age. We should all pray that the same thing that happened to Teri does not happen to Tina, for goodness' sake."

"You're right, dad," says Jake.

At the seventh inning stretch, Jake looks at Jon and tells him, "Go get us some chocolate. You fly, I'll buy."

"Sure," declares Jon.

Jon takes a ten-dollar bill from Jake and walks up the stairs, through the exit, and toward the concession stands. He waits in line for a few minutes, and purchases three candy items for seven dollars and twenty-five cents. As he turns to head back to this seat, he sees Cat going into the restroom, leaving Tina standing by herself, holding a popcorn and soda. Jon walks over and speaks to her.

"Hello again; it's good to see you two enjoying the game," says Jon. "I didn't know you like baseball."

"It's all right. Cat likes it more than I do," she replies.

They talk for a few seconds, and then Jon moves closer and speaks in a quiet tone, "My dad says we should pray that you don't end up pregnant like your sister. I sure hope you don't, Tina. I mean, you're just starting your life."

"What the heck, Little Jon!" says Tina angrily. "I can't believe you told me that. Why would you think I would let that happen? Who do you think I am? If I didn't know you and like you, I would kick you where it counts. Mind your own business. Good-bye!"

Jon sheepishly waves as he walks away. Before he enters the inside of the ballpark, he turns and sees Cat leaving the restroom, walking to Tina. Jon knows Tina is going to tell Cat what she just heard. Jon feels embarrassed, like he really shouldn't have been so nosy.

The Martee men enjoy the candy and the rest of the game. A full moon graces the horizon as they drive home.

Jon talks as they travel. "I saw Tina at the concession stand when I went to get the chocolate. I told her that my dad said we should pray for her, and why. She was not happy about it. I think I offended her."

"Don't worry about it, Jon," advises Dad. "She'll get over it."

"It bothers me because she has been my friend for so many years," replies Jon. "I should have kept my mouth shut."

"Dad's right, little brother—don't worry. If anything, maybe what you said will help her think right." says Jake.

Mom is watching TV when they get home. "How was the game? Did we win?" she asks.

Jon replies, "The score was eight to five. We hit three home runs in the eighth inning to come back and win."

"Did you see the moon?" Mom asks.

"Beautiful," replies Jake.

"Unreal," says little Jon. "We saw Tina Jones and her boyfriend at the game. Dad is worried about her getting pregnant like Teri."

"Are you serious?" asks Mom, looking at her husband.

"Yes, Martha, I am serious. You should see this guy Cat. He looks like a young Cary Grant," elaborates Dad.

"Wow, this I'd like to see," Mom replies with a grin.

"I'm serious, dear. After hearing about Teri, I was taken back by Tina's demeanor at the game," responds John. "What is wrong with young people, anyway? I'll bet you anything Tina ends up pregnant like her sister Teri."

"Don't speculate too harshly, dear. Tina might be smarter than you think," replies mother.

They talk more about Teri's future and the ramifications Teri's pregnancy will have for her little sister. After thirty minutes, Jake and Jon head upstairs to go to bed.

Martha stays on the couch and tells her husband, "I'm going to wait up for Jan. She called about an hour before you got home and should be here soon."

"OK, dear. I think I'll hit the hay," says John.

Jake takes deep breaths while he lays awake in bed. He cannot stop thinking about Teri and Tina Jones, and can tell his little brother is also concerned. Jake prays for the best for the Jones family. He thinks about Tina as a young mother, and envisions the situation as being positive, but Jake knows inside that she is much too young, and has much too much to look forward to before being a mother.

Jake peacefully falls asleep. He wakes in his dreams to the sight of Oswaldo, who is waiting for him on the top of the roof. They whoosh away and travel the now familiar path toward the gates of purgatory. As they pass through a Gate, Jake turns his head in all directions, gazing at the glory. They come to rest in the magnificent Lobby, and Ben greets them both. Oswaldo then waves goodbye as he whisks his platform away from the Lobby.

"Welcome back, Jake. We have another situation to address, my friend," explains Ben. "We are on a mission to save your little brother's friend, Tina, from an unplanned pregnancy, and reinforce the strength of motherhood throughout her family.

Ben elaborates further. "This is a highly anticipated topic. Motherhood's strength is second only to the power of the positive." After a short interlude of smiling scrutiny of Jake, he continues, "A strong mother has such a lasting influence in people's lives. The depth of this topic extends far beyond the conscious reach of man's knowledge. A mother's love is second only to our Creator's love for us. When all else fails, a mother's love will still be there. Thank goodness for mother's love, Jake. A mother's love is as strong as it is gentle. It is nearly indescribable. I cannot be more emphatic when I say its power is awesome. In many instances, the strength and memory of a mother's love becomes a strong defense for the L-S-S."

Ben hesitates, looks at Jake, smiles, and continues. "Today, the population of the earth is filled with many children of uncaring mothers. Don't get me wrong. Way too many mothers have no choice or chance because of their surrounding circumstances. They cannot give their children the care they deserve, even though they desperately want to. However, the percentage of mothers who leave their children just because they can get away with it, is growing at an alarming rate. Because defaulting fathers have been evident since the onset of man, a mother's duty is unquestionably put to the test. Mothers are not supposed to abandon their children, no matter what. Now, evil works any angle it can to coerce mothers of the world to believe it is not wrong to abandon their maternal duties. Not only is abandonment premeditated by evil; it is frightening how devastating are the results,"

Ben continues, "We are going to visit Tina's R-A-S and utilize the Red Cerebra M-C-U to travel onto her sister Teri's Highway. We hope Teri will help set her sister's mind right about her own poorly timed gestation.

"Let's get started," Ben tells Jake. "So far, your family is very fortunate. However, fortune cannot depend on luck," says Ben as he hesitates and readies himself. "This world is unfortunately, not perfect. Some families have loving parents; some don't. I guess there is no other way to explain it. Society has defined what is right, and the definition is mostly fair and proper. Straying from doing the right thing is wrong, but anymore, the right thing to do is not always reinforced, and vice-versa. This is unfortunate, and most of the time the results are sad. *Every* kid deserves a real chance in life. It is up to the parents and society, to make sure all children are treated properly."

Ben hesitates and takes a deep celestial breath, "This is an area where purgatory struggles to pinpoint blame. Relationships, feelings of love, and so many different emotions all combine to tax the Limbic Highway at many different locations and at many different velocities. We do not have accuracy in the Limbic Highway when it comes to love. This is due to all the variables, and the necessity to be complex. The Tryphus and Endocrine System, where these traits originate and are regulated, are very difficult to track and monitor when dealing with love and emotion. Still, the strength of motherly love is on the axis of man's emotion. And, even though the thoughts of motherly love are intangible, the beliefs and facts of motherhood are very real, and invaluable to man. The L-S-S cannot identify and pinpoint the whereabouts of motherly love, but we know it is there, and it is utilized without saying."

"A normal Limbic Highway is affected by the emotions of love in the Amy-G, the P-F-L, and the Tryphus. There is a physical difference between man and woman, which can be visualized at the approximate area where the Tryphus attaches the to Amy-G. Man's connection is brownish blue, whereas a woman's is pinkish. Besides the difference in color, a woman has a connection to the entrance of each of the Cable-Four, disguised throughout the Limbic Highway. These faded pink, indistinguishable roads, enable the entire Cable-Four access to motherly love," says Ben. "It's a phenomenon. We have talked enough about the intangibles of love."

Ben and Jake glide onto Ben's platform. They rise upward toward the Live G-A Hall, cruising past the vast walls of the Administrative. The platform comes to rest at the door of Tina's Virmory. They are greeted by Tina's G-A.

"Hi, Jake, I'm Rita, Tina Jones' Guardian Angel," says the girl.

"Hi, Rita, pleased to meet you," responds Jake.

"Are you ready for us, Rita?" asks Ben.

"Yes, sir," replies Rita, and begins. "Tina is very gifted. She has the potential to not only be successful, but also to be a very positive influence to her family and community. You can see her Disclosure Wing is full, bright, and steady. She has limited evil barb penetration and doesn't lie much. She tells the occasional white lie, so to speak, but she is not calculated. She is a vibrant teenage girl, who is highly influenced by her family, and close to becoming a victim of an unplanned pregnancy."

"The one area of her Disclosure Wing that is inconsistent, is in the Libido section in her Amy-G," says Rita.

"Surprise, surprise," says Ben. "Tina has been snowed over by her family so often, that she ignores the ramifications of an unplanned pregnancy, and believes that premarital sex is acceptable. 'If it happens, it happens,' is the give-in attitude. Tina is still highly impressionable, even naïve. So, we shall attack Teri's Highway in hopes of getting some sense into her brain and heart, which in turn, should lead to some solid, positive sisterly advice."

Butch shows up in the Red Cerebra M-C-U. Rita stays behind as the guys glide onto the deck. Ben stands at his console while Jake finds his spot on board.

"Good day, gents," Butch greets them.

"Mr. Butch, what's up?" replies Jake.

"Take us into Tina's R-A-S first, Butch," instructs Ben.

They head straight into Tina's R-A-S. Jake is starting to get used to the scenery, and while Tina's R-A-S appears as Jake would expect, it seems more feminine that Rickey's or his own. They veer off into the P-F-L and cruise smoothly through countless communities of healthy neural clumps and pools. The amazing purple patterns never cease to amaze Jake. Gradually, the communities on the right side of their pathway turn into shades of blue. They veer right and find themselves in the middle of Tina's Amy-G. Butch drops them to the lower rim.

"Look at the pinkish, tightly spun layer at the bottom of the real bright blue community over on the left. That is the gasket of motherly love coming from the Tryphus. This is the only place you can clearly see the gasket. Men have a gasket also, and it is a dull blue, as its function is not as useful as a woman's," says Ben.

The Red M-C-U rises up and comes to rest in the middle of the source of an unusually bright-blue community.

"Don't get too close to those clumps on the left, Butch—they are way too bright. You might create a large gap in the Highway if you barely touch them, which could prove dangerous. Call in some help, we need to cool her down," Ben tells Butch.

In a matter of seconds, a dozen green M-C-Us arrive on the scene and immediately extend their vacuum apparatus into the fray. Each M-C-U emits an electrical coolant into the heart of the clumps. Before long, the bright colonies are calming, and the community simmers back toward a normal sheen.

"That is better," says Ben. "Rita should have known Tina's libido is over-heating. Who knows how long she was going to last?" he says.

"Wow!" says Jake, still gazing at the battlefield under repair. "That was something new."

"Yes, the M-C-U has different functions besides sucking evil barbs off the Highway," Butch explains. "It cools, it heats, and it even chips away crystallized walls."

"It is time to go, Butch," says Ben. "Get us over to Teri's R-A-S."

The Red M-C-U wastes no time getting out of Tina's P-F-L. Jake looks behind and sees the blue of Tina's Amy-G turn into the purplish highway of the P-F-L. Seconds later, they fly through Tina's R-A-S and find themselves in the R-A-S of Teri Jones, Tina's sister. Butch quickly guides them to Teri's Virmory.

"Hi, guys, hi, Jake; I am Jenny, Teri Jones' Guardian Angel," says Jenny.

"Hi Jenny, it is nice to meet you," responds Jake.

"Is everything set Jenny?" Ben asks Teri Jones' Guardian Angel.

"Yes, sir," replies Jenny.

"Before we start Jenny, I need to talk," says Ben, who then looks at Jake. "When your little brother talked with Tina near the concession stand at the baseball game, he hit a nerve and really got Tina hot under the collar. She is quite upset. Not at Jon per se, but at her conditions at home. She has a con-science in other words. Her sister's pregnancy has turned their families already over crowded household, into further disarray. Tina appears torn over what is right or wrong. As we just saw, her Libido is fired up, while the rest of her system remains calm and normal. Sex is a strong option right now, as a way to vent her frustrations. Danger! Danger! Danger!"

Ben continues, "Tonight, Tina prayed for her sister, her parents and herself. She also prayed for every girl in the world in the same situation as her sister Teri. She feels the pressure of being put in a predicament like this, but she really does not know how to interpret what to do. Still, she possesses positive thinking and that teenage inquisitiveness, so thank goodness Jon approached her, because, here we are."

"OK, Jenny—please begin," says Ben.

"Teri's Cable-Four has had plenty of strength issues the last two or three years. We came up with about a dozen times when her P-F-L and Hypo-Bulbo showed obvious signs of irritation. The episodes related to her mother and father engaging in a second parenthood found the most damage in her Highway. Most of the time, Teri is very stable and amiable, but since she has had to deal with her sister's children living at home with them, her system shows signs of wear and tear. Teri has become torn between following through with a career on her own, away from her family, or taking the easy way out, succumbing to raising a family at an early age, and, possibly, temporarily living with her parents while doing so," explains Jenny. "We found six specific episodes of Teri's life that could help."

"Very good," says Ben. "Let us take a look."

After reviewing the episodes, Ben reviews two in particular a second time. In the meantime, the L-S-S has figured the location coordinates in Teri's P-F-L that need Limbic cleansing.

"We need to look at these specific moments in Teri's life again Jake. These could be stepping stones to success for the L-S-S," illustrates Ben.

They review a scene from three years ago.

"Melissa is gone," begins Ben. "She came to visit, got up in the middle of the night, and took off for Las Vegas, leaving her two toddlers at grandma and grandpa's house. Teri and Tina were excited and happy at first, but after a few days, harsh reality set in for everyone. Their already busy schedule has taken a turn for the busier. Teri can see the same, inundated look in her mom's eyes that she is feeling. She resigns herself to the fact that her mother would never allow her grandchildren to be raised elsewhere, and the burden will be bearable, yet a daily grind."

The next scene is Tina and Teri's mother collecting money from Melissa before going grocery shopping. Melissa does not want to spend her welfare check on her children and bills. They argue for quite sometime then Melissa throws the money at her mother and walks out for the evening.

"She will dispute finances many more times before leaving for good," says Ben. "During this memory the L-S-S has found obvious signs of occupation in the Hypo-Bulbo, as the mental equilibrium coordinating community is hiding numerous tainted pools. However, the heaviest occupied areas are in the P-F-L, and, as we found in Tina, the Amy-G is where most overexcitement is taking place," says Ben.

"We have got the coordinates, Ben," says Butch.

"Very good, let's continue on," agrees Ben.

The Red M-C-U jets back into Teri's R-A-S and continues into Teri's Basal-G. Their location is obvious to Jake as the orange hue of he Physical 4 surrounds them. He anticipates them approaching the Brocal and Somaesthetic Areas as he looks for the red background of the Thalamus. He notices slight faint showings of pink shimmers.

"Hey, Ben," asks Jake, "Do you see those pink shimmering streaks?"

"Good eye Jake. If you watch one area long enough, you might see them again. Teri is seven weeks pregnant and her motherly love has already begun reaching out to her Limbic Highway. The pink lights, which are rarely visible, are streaks of motherhood. It is beyond wonderful, isn't it?" questions Ben.

"Amazing!" answers Jake.

Butch swings over to the right side of the large pathway they are traveling. Sure enough, they pass the Brocal and Somaeshetic Areas with the red background of the Thalamus showing itself. They see nothing alarming and continue on, into the center of the Basal-G. The orange hue color turns to yellow as they approach the Healing Generator.

"We want to look at Teri's Healing Generator," says Ben. "All signs point toward the P-F-L and Hypo-Bulbo, but we need to make sure Cerebra has no major obstacles during dreamtime. Plus, we will get a better idea of where to look in the Hypo-Bulbo and P-F-L if we find pertinent dead pools in the Healing Generator."

The Red M-C-U wastes no time and heads directly into the middle of Teri's Healing Generator. The power is consistent, so Butch heads down front, deeper within the yellow communities. Eventually, they see darker colonies in front of them, and as they approach, Jake notices the brown outlines of several dead pool communities on both sides of their vessel.

"Good work Butch," says Ben. "Notice the dead pools on both sides of this section. We anticipated the ones on the left. That area positively stimulates Teri's Amy-G. No surprise that her Libido stimulator is tainted, but on the right, some digestive tissue sections in the Generator are weak. Teri has spent endless hours studying, but lately she has spent many hours sitting around watching T.V and eating instead of studying. Guess what she eats when she is a couch potato?" asks Ben as he looks at Jake and Butch. "That is right. Junk food."

The vessel continues throughout most of the main highway of the Healing Generator and scours the Caudate and the other three sections of the Phyical-4. All is well, so they head back to Teri's R-A-S and veer downward, through the passage into Teri's Hypo-bulbo. The bright red of the Thalamus turns to a light pastel green of the Hypo-Bulbo. Butch knows the coordinates of the digestive issue, and they approach the area in no time.

"Where is the back-up?" asks Ben.

"Right behind us, sir," answers Butch.

Fifty green M-C-Us line up in order behind their Red M-C-U. They move forward somewhat stealthily, and cruise past many healthy communities, all the while, readying themselves for the charge. Butch leads them into the beginning of the tainted parcels, and Jake sees black puffs of evil voraciousness every-where in front of them. A dozen of the green M-C-Us from behind scurry out in front on them, into the tainted communities, establishing a boundary amid the thick, black evil occupation. Jake feels a bit worried as they are surrounded by neural pool invasion. There is so much evil, the M-C-U's struggle at first sucking the barbs out of Teri's brain. However, Jake can tell the occupation is not as deep as Rickey Magerro's, and before long, and after a few intense moments, the M-C-Us rid the area of the high volume of evil barb occupation, and the intensity subsides.

"Holy cow, Ben!" cries Jake. "I was getting a bit worried."

"I know what you mean young man. We had no idea the infestation was so heavy, especially in the autonomic Hypo-Bulbo," answers Ben. "Thank goodness your Red M-C-U has priority."

Butch works his way up the community to where the rest of the M-C-Us are mending torn clumps. Their mission here has been accomplished. Ben motions to Butch, and the vessel heads out of the digestive section, onward, toward the Appurvesti.

"How was that Jake?" asks Ben. "I thought we did well for not expecting this. Teri needs to change her eating habits. The cleansing operation we just completed can only show short-term results, but it is the short-term, immediate results, we need for Cerebra's dream to go unobstructed. Now it is time to cleanse and repair her Appurvesti. This is not nearly as simple as the digestive area we just cleansed. It is more difficult to pinpoint mental equilibrium infestation, compared with bodily functions."

Within seconds they are within sight of the Appurvesti, which astounds the crew with its constantly changing colors and patterns.

"This is a bit deceiving, Jake, because the Appurvesti is not only located in the Hypo-Bulbo, but also crosses the Thalamus into the lower P-F-L. The changing colors are like that on purpose to act as a defensive mechanism to disguise the Amy-G area. The brilliant reflections throw the evil barbs and confuse them," explains Ben. "The Appurvesti is highly protected, because it is the main coordinator of mental balance within the Limbic Highway."

Traveling with forty or more green M-C-Us, the Red M-C-U makes its way across the Thalamus into the P-F-L. They find signs of strong evil occupation. They get used to the brightness and witness the M-C-Us starting to repair a hole when a wall blows open and evil hysteria sprints and weaves a circle around them. Ben instructs Butch to get them out of the area, immediately, and a dozen green M-C-Us guard the Red M-C-U and create a safe path for Ben, Jake and Butch to escape. The rest of the team stays and wages the necessary battle to contain and rid the enemy. As they high-tail it back into the heart of the Hypo-Bulbo and head toward Teri's R-A-S, Jake looks back at the Apppurvesti and sees monstrous clouds of fuming, chomping, disgusting blackness, readied for expulsion.

The try for an evil bulge was squelched. Evil's meager attempt to alienate the L-S-S during its mission was foiled, thanks in some part to the Red M-C-U.

"I know what you are thinking Jake," says Ben. "You want to know if the evil bulge would have succeeded if we would not have shown. Right?"

"Yes, Ben. You are amazing," replies Jake. "Tell me the answer."

"The evil presence was large, and it was in a tender, sensitive area. However, it takes a lot to influence a person enough to allow an evil bulge a free pass to the deepest fissures of someone's brain," says Ben. "This attempt we experienced is dangerous, and it shows on the surface with Teri's attitude of late. But, it is not the end of her world. She has millions of clean Limbic Highway roads in her system."

"Were we in danger, Ben?" asks Jake.

"You probably think we were because of how we quickly exited the scene. We ran not because we would be eliminated; we ran because we did not want to experience what happens if you are successfully attacked. What happens to us good guys is, we are expelled into the atmosphere. We then get back on the Thalamus of someone's Cable-Four and return to purgatory to start again. It usually does not take too long to return, but once in a while we run into a bit of friction in the atmosphere. We will talk about that later." They continue into Teri's R-A-S and pause.

"Teri is the one who was in serious danger. If the evil bulge succeeds in its goal, untimely death is often the result. Our Red M-C-U makes it possible for us to travel from Limbic Highway to Limbic Highway, maintaining M-C-U capabilities at all times. In this instant, we located the dangerous occupation and took care of business. However, we do not know if the Red M-C-U was noticed by evil. Evil is very cunning, and should it possibly detect a difference in the Red M-C-U, things could be difficult."

Butch adjusts the console as the vessel sits in Teri's R-A-S.

"What is the report from the P-F-L?" Ben asks Butch.

"They found more damage then expected, but they will give the clear within minutes," he answers.

Within seconds, Butch speaks, "All clear in the libido section of the P-F-L sir."

Ben speaks to Jake, "This is the last effort of the L-S-S before Cerebra's dream. Our estimates show that we should have success with the dream machine, and we will find out soon, my friend." He looks at the pilot. "OK, Butch, let us begin.

A dream Cerebra has created begins on the enlarged screen.

FIVE

Terri Jones' Dream

It is the day after aunt Chelsea's birthday party. Teri's sister Melissa and her boyfriend Ralph are at his cousin Witten's house for dinner. The night before, at the party, Ralph and Witten talked for nearly three hours after dinner, while everyone else danced and partied. At the party, Witten invited Ralph and Melissa over tonight.

After dinner, Witten serves a custard dessert with a tasty punch-flavored tea. Melissa has two cups, but she does not realize it was an aphrodisiac. Neither Ralph nor his cousin Witten will ever tell Melissa about the spiked tea.

This is the night when Melissa conceives her first child. Ralph and she will be married two months later, and their first child, Zachary, will be born seven months after their marriage.

Teri is now in her dream, talking with Tina. She is scratching her head at the facts she just witnessed. "Ralph is a rat," she says to Tina. "I feel so upset that Melissa was subconsciously coerced into having unprotected sex, resulting in pregnancy."

"Why did our sister leave her children and move to Las Vegas?" asks Tina.

"Because Ralph moved to live with his brother in North Carolina six months ago, leaving Melissa on her own, and she couldn't make it," replies Teri. "She struggled to make ends meet, and then hooked up with an old friend and got caught up with addiction. She slowly lost her grip on everyday bills and life. Eventually, she really had no choice but to leave her children at Mom and Dad's house while she gets some help."

They both agree with their mother that Melissa needs to clean up her act, without her children being directly subject to the problem.

Teri falls back in her dream. This time Melissa is at an AA meeting. Everyone at the meeting is standing, holding hands. Jim and Gwendolyn lead the gathering and ask everyone to close their eyes and pray for strength to heal.

After two minutes of silence, Gwendolyn breaks the quiet, "Did anyone else feel that strong motherly connection, like all of our mothers' spirits are floating among us? It was heavenly!"

Again she asks, "Did anyone else feel their mother?"

"Yes, I did," says a teary-eyed Melissa. "I miss my kids so much. I am such a loser."

Gwendolyn goes over to Melissa and gives her a hug. After the meeting, Gwendolyn and Jim talk with Melissa about the positive things in her life.

"That was surreal, Melissa," says Gwendolyn. "The feeling you felt—I felt it too. It was truly spiritual. It shows you care, you know. Things will always work out if you believe, and you believe, Melissa."

Melissa forces a smile, wipes the tears from her eyes and says, "Thank you for being a real friend."

The dreams Cerebra creates continue to register throughout Teri's R-A-S Cerebra. The next dream turns the influence to Teri's heroine, Princess Diana. Unfortunately—and Teri will witness this in her dream—the two-sided sword of the media not only spreads the good work of Princess Di, but also kills her.

Teri studied the works of the princess for years after her death.

Im the dream, it is 1997: Teri sits in the car outside a concert hall in Chicago. She is quite upset, because her friends talked her into driving three hours to see her favorite folk singer perform, only to find the singer cancelled earlier in the day because of a soar throat. Instead, a hard-driving, three-member Southern rock band takes center stage. Her friends enjoy the show inside while she sits in the car, wanting to be alone. While listening to the radio, Teri hears the news of the car accident that took the life of Princess Diana and shooks the entire world. She cries uncontrollably for nearly an hour.

Back in the present: Since Teri found out she is pregnant, she thinks about Diana's life all the time. She feels sad for Di's children and family, even though it has been over ten years since her death. Diana was forced out of her daily routine and eventually to her death by the paparazzi. The work and effort Princess Di gave to needy children all over the world is incomparable to her family's suffering. Teri admires Diana's peacefulness and ability to remain calm. It seemed as if nothing bothered her, but Teri thinks she must have hurt inside.

In 1997, Teri struggles with her emotions as she sits in the car. She listens to the circumstances and reasons for the excess speeding and the accident. She becomes livid with anger at the paparazzi. She closes her eyes to envision the accident and falls asleep, dreaming.

"Stop it right there," Ben tells Butch.

Butch puts the dream on hold.

"Princess Diana's Limbic Highway was pristine. There were no nagging evil occupations lingering in her brain. She was a focused individual. Her marriage and subsequent relations strained her life and family, but those circumstances were not influenced or skewed by evil influence. No, Diana was a wonderful human being who worked tirelessly and traveled untold miles to help the needy children of the world. She wanted kids to be loved. The issue, which led to her death, is where the evil barbs lurked. However Cerebra has found that the integrity of her life is so well illustrated, and so many people are internally moved by her death, that it is a very important, useful dream tool."

"Where did the evil lurk, Ben?" asks Jake.

"Evil finds many intangible methods to wreak havoc in the world," says Ben. "War is the strongest force evil brings to the table. We talked earlier about an individual's Limbic Highway during wartimes. As with an evil bulge, evil succeeds with strength in numbers, right?

"In war, humans are put in a tremendously difficult situation, which oftentimes they cannot control. Guardian Angels do all they can do to keep humans alert and ready to defend themselves during war, but the strength of military efforts far outweighs the potential of the individual."

Ben hesitates, looks at Jake over his glasses, and puts his arm around young Martee.

"Princess Diana's untimely death was brought on because the human pressure brought upon her was coerced by evil cunning. Evil has found a reliable host in the paparazzi. It found an area in the P-F-L that it can coerce to ignore the Tryphus and the sense of punishment, the feeling of guilt. Now that evil knows of this effective method, it thrives on the results. The paparazzi, with their snobbish, uncaring media-monger attitudes, have become a vile evil host with multiple tentacles. The glory of their stories far outweighs their human results. In other words, they do not care about a story's serious impact; they care only about their own gain. Not too surprising really, and they live below the belt, bush-league. In fact, this trait is much too rampant among man: Short-term gain, achieved at someone else's expense. The problem is not the individual; the problem is it has become a given among information thieves. Morals and ethics are vanishing ingredients in the recipe of success," finishes Ben.

"How can Teri change from this situation?" asks Jake.

"She is going to be among the frothing paparazzi the evening of the crash," elaborates Ben. "The blatant, unnecessary agony Princess Di suffers will positively influence the mode of thinking for Teri Jones, by prioritizing motherhood. Really, there is nothing more. Let us watch."

"Go ahead and let her roll, Butch," says Ben.

Butch makes the move and touches the button.

———•———

Teresa is having coffee and a pastry with her coworker Antoine. They have been chasing Princess Di for nearly three weeks. Today, they know Di's schedule and have the morning free to themselves, so they decide to see the Arc de Triomphe and do some shopping. The Champs Elysées is beaming with life this particular Saturday. The sun is out and the roads are dry. This is Paris. The traffic patterns are chaotic, and the lack of direction reminds Teresa of the bargaining that goes on at a street market. The noise surrounding them is of sirens, honking, yelling, and emissions.

The two of them sit at an outside table at the Café du Roi, having lunch and talking about their upcoming evening.

"I'd give anything to have the best photo tonight," says Antoine. "I mean, I'd do *anything* to catch her doing something exciting, wouldn't you?"

"Don't get too excited, Antoine," says Teresa. "We've put ourselves in a pretty position, and, barring unforeseen schedule changes, we will be in a group of less than ten when she leaves the hotel. You run interference, and I'll capture the world."

Teresa is from Rome, while Antoine lives in Naples. They were hired by the same company during the same week and have been working together for the past eight months. Antoine's uncle Lukas was a pioneer of the paparazzi. Lukas spent many nights behind bars because of his intrusive maneuvers. He also had more magazine cover photos than any other Italian photographer. Antoine wants badly to be half as successful as his uncle Lukas, but finds the competition to be nearly suffocating. Teresa has the same goals in mind as Antoine, but does not have his experience. However, she is cunning and diligent to her cause. The combination of his experience and her chivalry makes them an effective pair. Their egos exude vanity, sprinkled with intangible fear. They finish their coffee and walk down the boardwalk toward the parking garage that temporarily houses their vehicle. After lunch, they plan to hide themselves close to Princess Di's hotel until Diana leaves after dinner.

The inside information Antoine received says Diana is not going to fly to Egypt tonight. Instead, she will stay in Paris an additional two days, and then go to Switzerland for three days of speaking and skiing. Only then will she resume her affairs in Africa. This is contrary to what is printed in today's newspaper and listed on the web. However, this type of deceit has become common, as celebrities yearn for privacy.

Antoine and Teresa downplay what they are doing today, if and when they interact with their peers. They have become stealthy liars in an occupation that thrives on timing.

The afternoon sun settles behind the skyline of Paris, while Antoine and Teresa wait across the street from Princess Diana's hotel. They saw a slew of British limousines drive past the service entrance an hour ago. Everything is going just as Antoine was told.

Quietly, they are in their car waiting. Teresa has found the perfect parking spot adjacent to the hotel, barely out of sight of the service entrance. There is no way the limousine will leave through the front entrance. No way. This is supposed to be a secret. If Princess Diana does leave through the front entrance, Antoine and Teresa will be left in the cold, at least for this day.

"Are you sure you want to drive?" asks Antoine. "I have driven these streets at night before, you know."

"Yes, you told me earlier today, remember?" responds Teresa. "I am ready to drive, I can feel it."

"Regardless," says Antoine, "Let's get the job done."

"That's right, partner," says Teresa, testily.

Antoine gets a call on his cell phone and listens. He hangs up the phone and straightens his posture.

"They're getting ready to leave," says Antoine. "Are you ready?"

"You know it, buddy. I sure hope we get the edge," Teresa nervously replies.

"Zoot! Look over there," says Antoine.

Up ahead, Teresa can see five or six cars she knows are occupied by paparazzi. They anticipated some competition tonight, but no one else is supposed to know the time and location of Princess Di's exit. However, Teresa knows the other cars also anticipated the change, because of their experience of being foiled many times in the past.

"Oh, well, are you surprised?" asks Teresa.

"Darn. I thought we'd get a head start at least. We still have a good chance though. Be ready—you have to be aggressive," says Antoine.

"Just hang on," replies Teresa.

Suddenly, three identical limousines exit the service entrance, and speed onto the highways in three different directions. Antoine and Teresa watch as the paparazzi cars upfront chase after them. The middle limo screeches to a halt just in time to let two French-made sedans pass them, avoiding an accident. Teresa accelerates to keep up with the middle limo. She knows it is the one carrying the Princess.

They are in the far lane of six as they reach a speed of 100 kilometers an hour approaching an upcoming traffic signal. As the light turns yellow, she sees the brake lights of the cars in front of them and feels she is not going to make the light. Quickly, she veers sixty degrees to the left and hits the gas. She barely gets past three oncoming vehicles, also slowing for the light. She skids into the second lane and swerves into the far left lane as she straightens the car. The paparazzi in front of them, who are also speeding through the light, are three car lengths in front. The gas pedal is pushed to the floorboard, as they streak through the intersection.

The race is on. Teresa quickly catches up with the three paparazzi cars. The six lanes suddenly merge into three, and she barely sneaks into the third lane in front of two cars as the merge ends. They can see the lights of the limousine up ahead of them, but the limo is pulling away. The limo gets through the last light before heading into the tunnel ahead, but no one else could beat the red and get through the intersection. All four paparazzi come to a screeching halt, barely refraining from entering the intersection and certain damage.

"Damn it!" yells Teresa. "We had her, we had her, we had her!"

The light seems like it takes forever to turn green. As they approach the tunnel, they see nothing but brake lights and stalled cars piling up in all the lanes at the entrance. A middle-aged man is running out of the tunnel frantically waving his hat and shouting at the top of his lungs. "Accident, bad accident," he is yelling.

"What the heck?" says a puzzled Antoine. He sticks his head out the window and yells in French, "What's going on?"

They hear the man yelling, "The limousine crashed into the divider and two other cars slammed behind them. It is awful. Someone please call an ambulance!"

Two police motorcycles are in the vicinity and immediately are on the scene, keeping traffic and people from entering the tunnel.

"You better somehow hurry to the other side Antoine," says Teresa. "We have got to get a shot of that limo. Wow, this is terrible, but, we are here first. Call me when you get there," Teresa spews, with a cynical smirk across her face.

As Teri wakens in the car, the entire world begins to mourn the loss of Princess Di. She wipes her tears away and sings the words of a song she just made up.

Not to be political or trite
Never hints of ever losing sight
How she thought the world should be for kids

Wishing love for all of them
How can we not learn from her experience?
The price she paid, enough to teach a lesson
Thoughts of kindness, everlasting impressions
So many things she did for all the world

Can't you feel her South Africa?

Diana lives in our hearts, her memory's everywhere
Smiling through adversity
Showing children someone cares
The memory of her smile
Is what the world really needs
Why is it so difficult, to love your fellow man?

The things Di did for all of us, the real world
Were from the heart; peace can be attained
Through it all still the press hounded her
Just so the world could witness her pain
A shameful tragedy

Diana lives in our hearts
Her memory is everywhere
Laughing through painful times
Helping children suffer less
Sure hope her sons will be all right
Realize their mum was great
Wanting peace for all the earth
Though the media gave a hoot
Does anyone really care

Not to be political or trite

Teri dries her eyes and straightens her blouse as she prepares to go into the building and listen to music. The climax of her dream, along with her song and the cleansing of her tear ducts, have made her feel better. She can only think of how wrong it is that Diana cannot be a mother anymore, and that her children must miss her badly everyday. The world sure misses her, she thinks.

Teri mourns as she walks into the old church converted into a concert hall. She sees her friends leaning on a rail at the back left, just past the bar, and goes over to them. The music stops just as she arrives.

"Princess Di was killed in an accident in Paris today," she says.

Nobody says a word and the music resumes, leaving them with a numbed feeling, which rock n' roll played too loud will do.

———

Back in purgatory, Ben addresses Jake, "There you have it. If that doesn't inspire Teri, I don't think anything will. Look over here. Cerebra monitored the Limbic Highways of hundreds of paparazzi who followed Princess Diana. They all have one thing in common. Their sense of punishment by guilt is tricked into dormancy, and they justify their obtrusive, bordering-on-illegal ways. The attributing communities in their Gnostic Area are riddled with hidden evil occupations. Evil has twisted a specific population, the paparazzi, into ignoring their sense of shame and sense of right, by attacking their mental balance within pertinent communities. This in turn, enables evil to trick the Tryphus into complacency. It is the same principal as war, where mass confusion and hysteria within the Limbic System reign over the individual. Believe me, it frustrates the L-S-S."

"What about Teri and Tina?" asks Jake.

"Teri is definitely going to talk sense to Tina. She will never forget witnessing the senseless untimely death of Princess Diana and the shallow cause of the forceful paparazzi. With the cooling of Tina's Amy-G we accomplished earlier, and a good talking to from her best friend—her sister Teri—Tina will likely take to heart everything she hears. Even though Cat Becker might still talk her into premarital sex, Tina will not engage in tomfoolery without insisting on birth control. Thank goodness!" says Ben. "What we can do from the Live G-A Hall, is try to keep Tina on her toes when it comes to alcohol or drugs, substances that make it easier for Cat and soften Tina's free will. It sure is not easy," says Ben.

Ben floats their platform out of Teri's Virmory down to the Lobby, while he elaborates on what they just visualized. "It was essential to show you Princess Di's final hours, Jake. I know it is one of the worst personal tragedies of mankind, but knowing the roots of the issue can only help us as we strive for world peace. Of course, it also helps Tina and Teri Jones. Princess Di was much too resilient to be taken from earth at such an early age. Unforeseen disaster became evil's only viable catalyst to get Diana. Evil's barbaric demeanor and cunningness was utilized in the same manner as war, to suffocate the paparazzi's Limbic Highways."

Ben pauses, and then resumes, "If evil can use strength in mass of numbers to achieve usually unattainable goals, why cannot man use the same principle to achieve the goals of peace? We wish it that simple. Even though it seems like an unrealistic goal, influencing the masses is the way to go. Our goals become clearer each and every time you visit, Jake. In the future, we will strive to take the accomplishments we make from the individual area of action to a broader stage. Believe me, it is nothing but encouraging, my friend."

Ben smiles at Jake, "God bless you! I look forward to any and all adventures of the promising future."

"Thank you Ben, for everything," says Jake.

Jake glides onto Oswaldo's platform after it stops on the Lobby floor. The two of them salute Ben, and the mystical carpet exits purgatory. They glide through the magnificent arches of purgatory, through the celestial skies of outer space, into the earth's atmosphere, and safely into Jake's room.

He briefly wakens, and as he falls back in his own sleep, Jake thinks to himself, "What will tomorrow bring?"

(4)

Little Jon is up early attempting to make breakfast for his brother and himself. They are going to travel over an hour to a soccer game today, and Jon wants to show his brother he appreciates his effort of taking the time to take him to the game. The problem starts with the can opener busting before it got all the way around the top of the orange juice can, leaving Jon with frozen juice stuck in the wobbly cardboard tube. As he fumbles with the container, his mother walks in the kitchen, whistling a morning tune.

"What are you doing?" she asks.

"I am fighting with this darn orange juice container. I sure hope the game isn't this difficult," replies Jon.

"Here, give it to me. I'll show you a trick. I have had to open these buggers many a time," says mom.

Mom takes the container, slips the tip of a paring knife under the lid, and slowly cuts the metal lid off the top. She does not spill any, and beams a bit at her success.

"There you go, honey. Ready to squeeze into the jug," says Mom.

"Thanks, mom. But why can't we have fresh half gallons instead of frozen?" asks Jon.

"I know, they're more convenient, and taste better, but I got a good deal on frozen and couldn't pass it up. How about if we do both?" she replies.

"Fine with me," says Jon. "Too bad you and Dad can't come to the game today. We just have to win."

"You know your father and I would if we could. You buckle down and play your best, and you'll do just fine. I know you will. When are you leaving, and is Tommy Chock going with you?" asks mom.

"The game is at noon, so we are leaving in about an hour. Tommy and Jimmy Padilla are going with us. Jake is the best brother, you know that, Mom?" asks Jon.

"Yes, honey, I know," she answers.

Mom helps Jon make a simple, yet hearty pregame breakfast. They have slices of bacon, scrambled eggs with melted cheese, sourdough toast with Mom's homemade strawberry jam, slices of cantaloupe and banana, and of course, orange juice.

An hour passes by quickly, and they are finished with breakfast, ready to head to the soccer game. After finishing her chores, Mother sits at the table reading the morning paper with a cup of coffee in her hand. Jake stands at the kitchen sink, finishing a glass of water.

"You know your father and I will be gone until tomorrow around noon, right?" asks Mother.

"Yes, Mother, we know you aren't sleeping at home tonight," responds Jake.

"When do you think you will get home?" asks Mother.

"The after game snack barely touches the boys' appetite, so I think we'll stop somewhere for a good meal. I bet we get home around six or seven," says Jake.

"Do you need money?" asks Mom.

"I told Jon to tell the boys to bring a few bucks for a hamburger," answers Jake.

Mom hands Jake forty dollars and says, "Just in case."

"Thanks, Mom. You are the best," responds Jake.

"I will call you around eight to check in," says Mom.

"Sounds good to me. No question we will be home by then. Have a great time tonight," he tells Mother.

The boys get all their gear together. get in Jake's SUV, and head toward the Chock house. The day is overcast but dry.

"Did you bring everything? Water bottle, game jersey, cleats, and shin guards?" asks the older brother.

"I think so, let me check," says Little Jon. "Yep, even my shin guards, I am good to go."

"Where does Jimmy Padilla live?" asks Jake.

"He lives over by Goose Park, but I think he will be at Tommy's house when we get there," answers Jon.

'That would be nice," says Jake. "I don't think that I have seen Jimmy play, have I?"

"He's a pretty good player. His family just moved here from Arizona, and you can tell he played a lot of soccer. Didn't you see him play against the Stallions two weeks ago?" asks Jon.

"I missed that game, remember? Pam and I were taking a test that week-end," answers Jake.

"That's right. I forgot. Anyway, Jimmy is great for the team. He really passes well," says Jon.

Jimmy is waiting with Tommy on the porch when the guys arrive at the Chock residence. Tommy and Jimmy gather their bags and get in the motor vehicle.

"Hi, Tommy. Hi, Jimmy—this is my brother, Jake," says Jon.

"Hey, Jake," the two say in unison.

"Hey, Tommy. Good to meet you, Jimmy," says Jake as he looks over his shoulder.

"It is good to meet you too," responds Jimmy. "Thank you very much for taking us to the match today. Do you play soccer?"

"I played a few years. I like the game, but never had much exposure to it, like you guys. Do you have any brothers or sisters that play?" asks Jake.

"I've got two little brothers and one older sister. My sister played in high school, but not any more. My little brothers are in the seventh and fifth grade this upcoming year. They both play very well, but the youngest one is going to be very good," states Jimmy.

"Cool," says Jake. "What is the youngest one's name?"

"Miguel," answers Jimmy.

"From the sound of things, it is a good thing you are playing with us, especially today," says Jake.

"I cannot wait to get on the field," says Jimmy.

They drive the forty miles in the heavy weekend traffic. Fortunately, they left plenty early so they wouldn't stress if they met unforeseen distractions.

Jake quizzes Tommy a bit on his family situation. Everything seems to be working out for the Chocks. Tommy's dad has reappeared in their lives in a positive manner. Tommy's mother has already found another job, not as lucrative as her cannery job, but they get full health benefits, and she and her two kids can continue living at home. The Chocks will survive this year, and Tommy gets to enjoy his senior year of high school, as he deserves.

The traffic continues to be thick and fast as they approach their exit off the freeway. Jake is following a flatbed truck full of large wooden cants, and even though they are going nearly forty-five, people are passing them as if the SUV is at a standstill. The flatbed truck continues straight as Jake takes the gradual right turn of the off ramp. As they exit, a small black Honda pulls right in front of them and cuts them off, nearly running into their vehicle. Jake has to hit the brakes and almost slams into the car next to him on the right, also taking the exit. The three boys yell as they narrowly escape a collision and come to a stop. There is a chain of screeching behind them, and surprisingly, there is no loud fender popping. Jake puts the car in gear and continues off the exit ramp. Petrified, he pulls into the parking lot of the first gas station they come to.

Jake turns off the car, takes a deep breath and asks, "Is everyone OK? I am so sorry to scare you guys. Did you see that idiot?"

"It's OK Jake. You did a great job," says Tommy. "I bet that dude is part of that racing gang who try to be like that movie. They are so stupid. Who will die next, right?"

"That dude Tosh from our physics class has a souped-up Honda. Is he part of them?" asks Jon.

"I think so. My brother Mark knows that Tosh's brother is a member. Mark told me about it. They race for money and pride, and sometimes only pride. They should take it to a racetrack, but cannot pull the idea into reality, because of too much red tape and money involved," says Tommy. "I think they are so addicted to the excitement that it's rubbing off on their daily driving habits."

"I thought for sure we were going to wreck," says Jimmy. "Did you see the other dude on the right?"

"No, I didn't see him, but I figured someone was there. What I was mostly worried about was getting nailed from behind," says Jake. "Thank goodness we are all OK."

Jake composes himself, and they all get back in the car, buckle up, and continue on to the soccer game.

At the game, Jake mingles with the parents and other fans on the sideline. The action on the field is back and forth, fast and furious, and the score is zero to zero at halftime. After the halftime talk, Jon gives Jake his empty water bottle.

Before Little Jon runs on to the field, Jake says, "Pretty good first half, Jon-Jon. They could have scored twice on you, but they didn't. Now, you should get a chance or two. Give Jimmy the give-and-go as much as you can. He's too fast for them, I think."

"I'll tell him," says Jon as he heads onto the field.

"Go get 'em, little buddy!" encourages Jake.

The second half remains scoreless for the first twenty-five minutes. While Jake enjoys the game from the sidelines, he overhears a woman talking about one of her daughters getting into an accident. Apparently, someone forced the daughter off the road, and she hit a tree. She wasn't killed, but she broke her leg and scarred her arm and shoulder. The daughter says a speeding, small dark car, with tinted windows, forced her off the road.

Jake joins the conversation. "We had the same thing happen to us on the way here. Fortunately, we didn't hit a tree or anything."

Jake introduces himself to the people around him and tells them the story. They all agree these young fools are criminals and extremely dangerous. There is no place on the highway for speed games.

During the second half, Jon and Jimmy tried the give-and-go two times with no success. Finally, with about fifteen minutes left in the match, Tommy makes a nice steal and pushes the ball to Jimmy. Jimmy passes it to Jon, who is bringing up the middle. Jon one-touches the ball, perfectly leading Jimmy toward the goal. Jimmy controls the pass in full speed and races to a one-on-one encounter with the opposing goalkeeper. The keeper comes out of the box toward Jimmy, but Jimmy easily jukes him to the left and kicks the go-ahead goal into the net. All his teammates and the fans on the sidelines are ecstatic and enthusiastically applaud the "pretty" goal. The game is very tight for the final fifteen minutes, as Jon's team barely keeps the opponents from scoring four separate times. It seems like an eternity to Jake while he watches. Twice, Jon's goalkeeper had to make great saves. In the end, Jimmy, Jon, and Tommy are the stars, and their team advances in the playoffs.

On the way home, the car is full of excitement. The boys are getting rowdy, when Jake notices some vehicles in the rearview mirror, quickly advancing through traffic.

"Watch this, you guys. Look to the left at these dudes flying by," Jake says in a loud voice.

The boys stop the ruckus and watch as an orange muscle car and dark Honda fly past at outrageous speeds, cutting in and out of traffic.

"They must be going close to a hundred," says Jake. "What a couple of fools. All it takes is one car in front of them to suddenly change lanes, and boom!"

They watch as both speeding cars hit the brakes hard to avoid a truck changing lanes.

"See that?" points out Jake.

There is no accident, but everyone in the car is nervously reminded of the close call before the game. The noise in the SUV settles, as Jake take the next off-ramp to stop for dinner. He knows everyone is hungry, and at this point, everyone, including himself, would not at all mind getting out of the car.

After they sit down at a booth, the speeding controversy conversation continues.

"One of the parents told me her daughter was in an accident yesterday, when someone in a small speedster ran her off the road," says Jake.

"I heard that," says Tommy. "It was Tami Grace."

"Really?" asks Jon. "Is she OK?"

Jake replies, "She broke her leg and got scraped up, but she is going to be all right."

"Wow," says Little Jon. "I just saw her the other morning. I am sure glad she is going to be OK. Do you know who she is, Jimmy?"

"Tami Grace? I do not know that girl," he answers.

"Anyway," continues Jake, "Let's have something to eat. I'll bet you guys are hungry."

The three soccer players agree in unison.

Jake pitches in the forty dollars Mom gave him, so they could all enjoy a nice steak dinner with all the fixings. It was well worth it after such a glorious victory.

By six forty-five, Jake and Jon are at home and have settled into their respective routines. Jon has showered and is playing video games in his room, while Jake is downstairs watching TV. After a bit, Jon joins him with some popcorn.

At eight-thirty the phone rings. Jon answers and tells Mom all about the soccer game and his nice pass to Jimmy leading to the game-winning goal. He also tells his mother about the steak dinner afterward, and the near accident on the way to the game. Nearly five minutes later, Jon tells his mother goodnight and hands the phone to Jake.

"Hi, Mom," says Jake. "How is your dinner party?"

"Well, it is very comfortable. The food is excellent and the people are really nice. There are just too many of them," Mother says with a chuckle. "Your brother told me about your near accident. Who was that idiot who pulled in front of you?"

"I don't know, mother. It happened so fast, it sure shook us up," replies Jake.

Mother says, "I'll bet it did. You guys were lucky. Your father and I got caught up in traffic just after an accident on the way here. I am sure it is going to make the news on television tonight. You should look for it."

"What happened?" asks Jake.

"A delivery van ran over an old lady in a cross-walk. Well, it turns out the driver of the van is the daughter of a Washington congressman. Not only that, the congressman is close to being indicted for tax fraud, so the media is all over the story," says Mother. "I guess the walk sign wasn't lit when the lady was hit, and the driver had a green light. The driver was wearing headphones and didn't see the old lady."

"Was she killed?" asks Jake.

"No, but she is in critical condition," replies mom. "It really is turning out to be a big deal because there are so many pedestrian accidents lately, and because her father is a senator. Anyway, watch for it on the local news. We saw the cameras on us a couple of times, so you might see us on TV."

"I will mother. What time should we expect you tomorrow?" he asks. "Your father wants to visit a local museum before we head home, so I bet it is closer to two o'clock. Is that OK?" asks Mom.

"Of course. Say hi to dad," responds Jake.

"Thanks for everything, Jake. Call me if you need anything," says mom. "Good night, boys."

"Sure, mom. Good night," replies Jake.

Jan decides to stay at Judy's, and Jon is tired, so he goes to bed early. Jake pours himself a cold glass of water, peels a mandarin orange to snack upon, and stays up to watch the news. Sure enough, he finds that the story of Senator Jessport's daughter hitting a pedestrian with her delivery van is the second news item of the night.

Anita Jessport is the daughter of Ohio state senator Jeffrey Jessport. Jessport is up for reelection and is under investigation for tax evasion. His case has been drawing national attention, and now his daughter has put him into an even brighter media spotlight. The story ends with the announcer stating there will be further coverage of this story on the national news recap show immediately following the local news.

Jake's curiosity is heightened, especially after the day they had on the road. He proceeds to watch the whole ten-minute segment, and then rewinds the DVR machine and watches it again. What catches Jake's interest is that he wonders who is really to blame. Mrs. Fischer walked against a wait signal, while the driver turned legally through a green light. Was Mrs. Fischer already walking before the light turned green? Why was Anita Jessport not paying attention? How far will this case go? Will it affect Senator Jessport's case and career? What about Mrs. Fischer and her family? Should she be prosecuted for being in the crosswalk at the wrong time?

After the news, Jake watches twenty minutes of a network talk show, turns off the TV and goes upstairs to bed. While he lies awake, Jake worries about Mrs. Fischer.

"What was she doing crossing the street during a wait signal? Surely she is no criminal. She was probably daydreaming or something," Jake thinks to himself then falls asleep.

He wakes in his dream to Oswaldo on his platform.

"Mr. Jake! So good to see you again," Oswaldo greets him.

"It is my pleasure as well, Oswaldo," replies Jake.

They jet upward, through the atmosphere into outer space. Even though Jake has been here before, he is in awe as they head for the gates of purgatory.

"Do you ever get tired of the scenery?" asks Jake.

"No way, Jake. I never get tired of anything," replies Oswaldo.

Before long, Oswaldo glides through the gates of purgatory and sets the platform down in the lobby. Ben is waiting, standing next to his platform.

"Hello Mr. Franklin," says Oswaldo as the platform comes to a stop, enabling Jake to join Ben on the Lobby floor.

"Good day Oswaldo," replies Ben.

"Thanks, we will see you again," says Jake as Oswaldo whisks away from the Lobby.

Ben and Jake stand together on Ben's platform and talk about Jake's visit.

"How is it going, Jake?" asks Ben.

"Good, thank you Ben."

"You really got shaken up today. Plus, your mom and dad were shaken up as well. My goodness! The good thing is we have an important issue in the spotlight that needs to be addressed. And with you, we have the medium to accomplish some good. Good not just for the individual, but this time, for the whole," says Ben.

"Did you see what nearly happened to us?" asks Jake.

"Yes I did," answers Ben. "Thank goodness you did not get detained. Jimmy's goal was such a beauty, it would have been a tragedy if you guys could not have made the game because of a car accident. Seriously though, road problems have become such an issue for man. Evil knows the damage automobiles create, physically and mentally."

Ben elaborates, "It comes back to the same old saying: 'The more people there are, the more idiots there are.' Evil takes advantage of this fact, and road rage has become commonplace. It is a serious problem."

Ben adjusts his lenses and puts his arm around Jake. "The Fathers and Leaders have had a large input preparing the laws that have been established. The framework protects the driving population as a whole. However, individually, there are things purgatory can do to protect people behind the wheel and help them avoid accidents.

"We can initiate alertness by influencing thought with similarities. You know, like hearing a song on the car radio of an artist you had not heard for years, only to remember hearing the same artist earlier in the day. Also, drivers gain insight when they drive by a billboard and it triggers something in the brain.

"We can coerce a direction change or a lane change using adrenalin to coerce peripheral thought. It's kind of like the feeling of knowing someone is there without having heard or seen their presence.

"We can also assist in destination thinking. If we know of a dangerous driver driving toward us, we can kindly get their attention, or introduce an idea of an alternate road. The G-A is always there for the human, but when it comes to driving a car, the Highway is heightened, and the G-A utilizes aspects and gestures available to assure awareness. All in all, it is a righteous system, and when properly enforced, the method works.

"However, too many times the victim's rights are not protected, and the lack of proof allows the accused too much leniency. Offenders think this leniency justifies illegal action behind the wheel. Evil barbs, in turn, conjure methods using the leniency to hide within dormant, or seldom used neural communities, and road rage has become a daily activity. Quite ugly I may say," says Ben. "There will be a major court decision at the end of this case. A decision that will influence how our courts and people treat traffic laws."

Ben stops and stretches.

"We are going to visit the Virmory of three different road-raging drivers. We hope to find a pattern that will assist Cerebra to influence people making important final decisions. The method of getting these people to be involved is going to be executed by you," Ben tells Jake. "You will see what I mean."

Ben adjusts the console of the platform, and the men ascend into the heights of purgatory. They quickly pass through the Admin Area to the Live G-A Hall, stopping at a familiar place—Wendall Chock's Virmory. Waiting for them is Percy, Wendall's G-A.

"Hi, Percy, good to see you," says Ben.

"Hi, Percy, we've been talking about you," says Jake.

"Hi, guys. I hope it has been good," replies Percy.

"Are you ready for us?" asks Ben.

"Yes, sir, Mr. Franklin," says Percy. "We have run through countless memories of Wendall driving his construction truck to and from jobsites. The first year he was away from his family he was not too bad, but the more time passed, the more intense his road rage.

"The reasons he gets so mad are many. The first reason is that his Appurvesti lacks leadership. Wendall never got to be the captain of anything. Not the baseball team or the spelling bee squad—nothing—and he was always under intense pressure from his overbearing mother. We can see a distinct misfiring in the Appurvesti, as seen in the Disclosure Wing. The Appurvesti lacks continuity. The Gnostic Area does not connect with the Appurvesti nearly 20 percent of the time it is supposed to, leaving mental imbalance in the wings. Wendall ignores his conscience while he drives. He has many pestering evil colonies scattered throughout his P-F-L, which allow Wendall to believe over-aggressive driving is OK.

"There are other signs of P-F- L contamination inside of Wendall. His vanity proves that. The continual exploitation of community rights, proves there is more evil contamination in the behavioral pattern areas of the P-F-L. These occupations tend to dull the Tryphus, allowing Wendall's brain more justification to ignore any sense of guilt or common sense when he is behind the wheel. However, the bottom line is that Cerebra and the L-S-S are confident our studies have revealed the correct sections of contamination, which, after the L-S-S does their duties, will enable the two of you to complete your endeavor," concludes the long-winded Percy. "Wendall's road rage is an average example of how the driver convinces himself he is not doing anything wrong. Evil barbs have coerced complacency in certain intangible areas of his Limbic Highway."

"Very good, Percy," says Ben. "Wendall's aggressive behavior behind the wheel, is a result of the overbearing, brash attitude he attained from his early years of being berated by his mother."

"One Virmory down; two to go."

Ben directs their platform to another Virmory, up dozens of levels from Wendall's. They come to a stop at a doorway, and are greeted by a male figure.

"Jake, this is Hayes, Steve Magerro's G-A," says Ben.

"Hi, Hayes," says Jake. "So, you're Rickey's brother's G-A?"

"That's right. Someone's got to do it," replies Hayes lightheartedly.

"Go on then, Hayes," says Ben.

"Steve is a bad driver no matter what mood he is in. He is a mean driver when he is not in a good mood. The problem is that being in a good mood usually means being intoxicated. Thus, his road rage occurs nearly every time he gets behind the wheel. Now, Steve's Tryphus loses contact with the Amy-G during drunk driving episodes, and his driving habits can get really messy. The Amy-G gets way too hot, the Caudate and Putamen lose elasticity, and the Tryphus loses contact. The alcohol does not give the L-S-S a chance, and the G-A is forced into intense concentration to avoid disasters. We all know what can happen when alcohol makes people out of control," says Hayes. "The Tryphus losing contact with the Amy-G happens all the time with alcohol or drug abuse."

Ben intervenes, "This is a good example of what the Limbic Highway does, when the sensitive areas of the P-F-L become too intense for the Tryphus to handle. It is called 'phussing.' Being 'phussed' means that information, which is supposed to travel through the Tryphus for measure of truth, is unable to access the Tryphus because it is numbed by drugs or alcohol. Instead, the information bridges back through the Thalamus to its pertinent area without Tryphus interpretation. This non-truth-metered movement goes against the grain of the Thalamus, and because the information is tainted, it causes undue wear and tear on the system, especially over time. It happens way too often nowadays. Substance abuse isn't the only thing that causes 'phussing.' A person who constantly talks and lies without thinking is another example. The Tryphus cannot handle the constant disregard, so the bridge through the Tryphus closes and the information goes unchecked through the Thalamus, slowing the system."

"The obvious conglomerate of all these negative attributes is the habitual liar," continues Hayes. "Habitual liars are so blatant, they are constantly 'phussed.' Eventually, the Tryphus is completely ignored and you cannot believe a thing they say. Finally, a G-A cannot distinguish 'phussing' in the Disclosure Wing. All we can do is speculate when someone is 'phussed.' But, once you get the hang of it, you can almost always tell. So Jake, do you see the problem here? The Tryphus is the 'truth meter' of man, and it has intangible qualities that cannot be read in the Disclosure Wing. Habitual lying eventually tires the Tryphus, so the Limbic Highway creates a pathway to avoid the Tryphus, steering away from the continual guilt it would otherwise exude. This wears on the system terribly."

"Go ahead, Hayes, what else?" asks Ben.

"That's about it, Ben," replies Hayes. "We found many different dead pool areas all through Steve's Cable-Four, but, we've only talked about ones that truly pertain to Steve's road rage. He is either intoxicated, or, if he is sober, he is impatient because his P-F-L heats up too easily."

"Very good, Hayes," says Ben. "Two down, one to go."

Ben's platform heads back into the thick of the Live G-A Hall and weaves in and out of colorful hallways until it stops at a doorway occupied by a familiar face.

"You remember Rita, Tina Jones' Guardian Angel," says Ben.

"Hi, Rita," replies Jake.

"Hello, Jake, good to see you again," says Rita.

Rita spent her life in Philadelphia. Her genetic makeup is similar to Tina's, and they kind of look alike. Plus, Jake can see a distinct likeness to Tina's sister Teri in Rita's mannerisms.

"Tell us more about Tina," instructs Ben.

"Tina's Amy-G area is our main concern for her driving habits. She can't slow her hormonal highway, which operates slightly above normal for a girl her age. The concern is that her daily environment contributes to her attitude of recklessness behind the wheel. Not only does her home environment affect her demeanor, but also the power of the media steers her attention toward glamour and sex. Sometimes it steers people into a different, dark realm, but not Tina. She enjoys the limelight and excitement. Her terrible driving is not fueled by anger or hate, but rather by delirium, and by the fact she does not take it seriously. The L-S-S and G-A have a difficult time tracking seemingly innocent trouble because the disturbance is likely in the intangible Amy-G. However, the magnitude of what damage can be done with an automobile warrants any and all efforts of the L-S-S to avoid the potential harm." Rita takes a breath, "We know the disturbance is in the Amy-G, and we know it is almost impossible to pinpoint the location, but it is worth the effort, because once in, we can do some good when she is behind the wheel."

Ben interrupts, "Tina is full of life. She is very popular and hangs out with the 'cool' crowd at school. She has the mental ability to pursue a professional career. What we worry about, and this happens all the time, is there are too many mediums and avenues from which to choose. The constant barrage of decisions sometimes confuses a person as to which direction to travel is best for them. Unfortunately, many people do not find their best road to travel until it is too late. Go ahead and continue, Rita."

"Tina worships her sisters," says Rita. "The problem is, her oldest sister Melissa, has created a less than desirable situation because she abandoned her two children at Tina's house. Tina and Teri have to help their mother everyday with the kids. Teri is the same age as Jake's sister Jan, and a big influence in Tina's life. Tina does not mind helping, but she is quickly getting real tired of it. Plus, Tina can tell her mother is working too hard at her age to raise two more kids. All the factors add up to bother both girls daily."

"And as we know, Teri is pregnant," says Ben. "Go ahead, Rita."

"Teri and Tina have gotten closer since Melissa's kids have moved in to their residence. They talk about guys, being a mom, their future, and a lot of things. Teri has been going out with Jeremy Brown for over a year, and Tina just started going out with Cat. Teri told Tina that she loves Jeremy and they have been having sex for the last four months," explains Rita. "This excites Tina, as the two of them converse about everything."

Ben intervenes,. "Add all of these factors together, sprinkle in a little adult resentment, and Tina is like Ben-Hur when she gets behind the wheel. Sometimes, it's almost as if she goes too fast on purpose," says Ben. "She puts too much emphasis on such an innocent daily task."

They all pause for a moment.

"*Ben-Hur*—what a senseless waste of life filming that movie," says Ben. "Thanks, Rita," says Ben as they wrap up their visit.

"Now we are going to take a trip through Tina's Amy-G, and see if we can find the correlating connection to her Tryphus, which could pinpoint and confirm the cause of her road rage," says Ben.

Butch arrives on cue. Rita joins Ben and Jake for their journey. Within seconds, the Red M-C-U leaves Tina's R-A-S and heads into the purple world of her P-F-L. Jake notices healthy, vibrant neural communities as they venture toward her endocrine headquarters. Thousands of purplish communities later, they begin to see the blueness of the Amy-G. Butch heads for the brightest colonies he can find. He veers in and out of normal clumps, when he reaches a community pulsating at a much brighter degree than the rest.

"This is the spot, Butch," says Ben. "Do you know what area this is, Rita?"

"Her libido," she answers.

"Correct," replies Ben. "What a big surprise, right? Anyway, Tina is pumped up. The activities in her system are showing bright and overpressurized in the corresponding neural colonies. She has been talking and thinking about sex a lot lately. Additionally, her hormones are very active," says Ben.

"Which ones?" asks Jake.

Rita elaborates, "In the female, the pituitary gland is where female growth and activity is induced. The extremely bright sections we see correlate with her pituitary. Tina is young, but not too young, if you know what I mean."

"We know what you mean, Rita," says Ben. "The effort to utilize the information the Amy-G gives us is arduous. The endocrine system cannot be thoroughly tracked or pinpointed in the Disclosure Wing, or in memory. The most efficient method is for the L-S-S to visually inspect the section in question. This takes time, effort, equipment, and soul power. Because it is such a daunting, never-ending task, many times without conclusive results, the L-S-S cannot afford to monitor the Tryphus-Amy-G connection all the time. The exercise simply lacks efficiency. In other words, the endocrine system is intangible territory for the L-S-S, because the system's imperceptible qualities reveal the difficult efforts required to follow the system's path. Keep on going, Butch," says Ben.

Butch maneuvers them through the section of Tina's Amy-G up to the dark purple region of the Gnostic area.

"There, up to the left, can you see the lackluster communities?" Ben asks.

"I see them," says Jake.

"They are a classic example of a lack of respect for elders. We see it a lot with extended families living together. Between diminished personal care, and the jealousy of competition, Tina lacks respect for her elders. She respects her parents when she is with them, but otherwise she lacks respect," explains Ben.

Ben saves the coordinates of their recent visits into Tina's Limbic Highway, and instructs Butch to take them back to Tina's Virmory.

Butch drops his passengers at Rita's door and bids them good-bye.

Ben, Rita, and Jake continue to talk.

"Very good, Rita," says Ben. "We will absolutely use this information to find the right dream for the magistrate. The coordinates should also help the L-S-S clean other Highways. We will see what happens. Keep an eye on Tina's hormonal highway, Rita; you might need to send the L-S-S back into her Gnostic Area to cool her temper down. Keep us posted, OK?"

"You got it, Mr. Franklin," replies Rita.

Ben and Jake glide onto Ben's platform and return to the lobby of purgatory.

Ben explains to Jake, "Well Jake, we did what we set out to do. We know specific areas of concern when addressing road rage. Now, we need to contact the judge of Mrs. Fischer's trial and get him to pray, which will open his R-A-S. Then, we can access his R-A-S through your R-A-S Jake, and influence his thoughts."

"How do we get him to pray?" asks Jake.

"How do *you* get him to pray is a more appropriate question, Jake," answers Ben.

"You will remember my guidelines, Jake. You will not remember it was me who gave them to you, but you will remember them," he continues.

"You must study this case from the onset. Your best method is to follow it by watching the news and accessing the Internet website that covers the courtroom proceedings. Also, you will know when the timing is right to contact the judge. Believe me, you will know. The way you will contact him is either in person, by phone, or by e-mail, but we are pretty sure that you will be sending the judge an e-mail to get through. You will find out eventually," finishes Ben.

"Are you sure this is going to work?" questions Jake.

"You will be here with us when the time comes to answer that question," says Ben. "We will have it all together the next time you visit. Good luck, Jake!"

"Thanks, Ben. I—I guess I need it," Jake replies.

Oswaldo picks Jake up at the Lobby, and they swiftly exit purgatory through the magnificent arches. While they ride, Jake asks Oswaldo about his life.

"What do you do all day?" asks Jake.

"What do you mean?" replies Oswaldo.

"I mean, when you are not picking me up or taking me home, what are you doing?" asks Jake.

"I am utilized in different ways. I used to be a G-A, but since my human passed away, I mostly operate an M-C-U for the L-S-S. I guess I am pretty good at what I do because I was chosen to be your courier. We have battles everyday on Highways all around the world. Did you know that? Some people battle all day long. Their lives are cut short because their system cannot handle so much negativity. So, I move around from person to person, depending on where the intense battles are being waged. There are quite a few of us who are pretty good pilots, and as you know, as time moves on and the pioneer video game experts join us in purgatory, the more skillful the G-A who operate M-C-Us will become. That's kind of neat—a natural way to improve the system. Believe me, we need all we can get," finishes Oswaldo.

"Would you like to take a journey with us on the Red M-C-U?" asks Jake.

"Whoa, don't get me going! That would be fantastic, but I don't think Ben would go for it. The Red M-C-U is for some very serious dealings, not to be used frivolously," says Oswaldo.

"I don't know. I'll check it out for you," says Jake. "What else do you do? Do you visit Cerebra?

"Being a M-C-U pilot is a never-ending task," says Oswaldo. "That fact is pretty obvious, as every second of every moment is utilized to keep the system running smooth. We never get tired, bored, grouchy, or anything. It is being alive where you feel, grow and experience all the emotions of corporeal human existence."

"Yes, I have visited Cerebra. All G-As visit Cerebra before beginning their duty," adds Oswaldo. "How can I describe it? You've seen it, Jake—the entire purgatorial universe thrives on Cerebra. It is indescribably wonderful, isn't it, Jake?"

"Very well put," replies Jake.

They say their good-byes, and Jake is safely back home, surrounded by the warmth of his bed.

John and Martha get home Sunday around two o'clock, just as Mom assumed.

As soon as they walk in the door, Little Jon gets up and tells them, "We saw you on TV this morning. Twice! Dad was talking to a cop, and you were pointing at something while talking to somebody standing next to the car. It was cool, mom. Whom were you talking to?"

"Let me see, when your father was talking to that nice policeman, I was chatting with those people from New Jersey. They were across the street having a bagel and coffee when Mrs. Fischer got hit. They didn't see it happen, but looked immediately after hearing the screams. They were very friendly."

"Did you get their name?" asks Jake.

"Why yes, let's see, it was Kenner—Lillian and Tyrone Kenner, from Piscataway. She embroiders like I do," answers Mother.

"Tell us about it, Mom," says Jake.

"Help us get our bags first, boys."

The boys empty the car while Mom and Dad organize themselves. After a few minutes, Mom and Dad settle in the living room, where Jon and Jake join then in front of the television. Jan is at a friend's house.

Mom turns the television down and resumes her account of the events of the day. "We were there right after it happened, and if we would have been there thirty seconds earlier, we would have seen that lady get hit. I feel so sorry for that poor lady," adds Mom with a sigh. "Anyway, we got there just as the driver got out of the van. That poor lady was sprawled out in the middle of the street, and there were groceries and packages strewn everywhere. She must have flown ten feet out of the crosswalk, and it looked like she hit her head pretty hard. Anyway, the driver was a young girl with headphones draped around her neck. I think she was in a bit of shock because she looked stunned while she stood there watching. Fortunately, two cop cars were at the stoplight two blocks down, and they took control of the scene immediately. We were lucky because after they asked us a few questions, and took our information, they let us through. I heard on the news traffic was backed up for hours. I feel so sorry for that poor old lady."

"What happened to her?" asks Little Jon.

"They say she is in critical condition," answers Mom.

Jake intervenes, "I watched the news this morning. Mrs. Fischer died in the early morning hours."

"Oh, that is just terrible," cries Mother.

"That's not all," says Jake. "The driver didn't have insurance."

"Oh, my," says mother.

"How bad is that?" asks Jon.

"It's pretty bad," says Jake. "People who drive without insurance put everything they own at risk when in an accident, no matter if they were not responsible or not."

"And sometimes their relatives can get dragged into serious settlements," says dad.

"Now, Mrs. Fischer, Margaret is her name by the way, has a case against the driver, Senator Jeffrey Jessport's daughter," says Jake. "Well—I mean, her family has a case. It is bad that Ms. Jessport was going through the intersection too quickly, wearing headphones, and not paying attention, but no insurance is brazenly illegal. This could get quite interesting."

The rest of the day the family spends enjoying their lives after a busy weekend, with Monday on the horizon.

On the Sunday evening news, they find that Anita Jessport is accused of second-degree manslaughter, and the Fischers have filed a wrongful death suit against the Jessport family. The results of the Jessport manslaughter hearing, which starts immediately, will have significant bearing on the Fischer lawsuit.

Jake is not sure what the outcome will be, as Mrs. Fischer stepped into the crosswalk at the wrong time. Her arms were full of parcels and she could not see to her left, but at the same time, the van proceeded through a green light, and the driver, who was wearing headphones, did not see Mrs. Fischer.

The hearing begins as the prosecution presents a dozen eyewitnesses from the scene, each witness going through a rigorous one-on-one question and answer. The defense cross-examined each eyewitness, trying to show Mrs. Fischer's reason for neglect. They tried hard to prove that no matter the circumstances, when Mrs. Fischer entered that crosswalk, she was asking for trouble. They also made a thorough presentation of Anita Jessport's insurance records to date. They argued that Ms. Jessport had her insurance certificate with her, and that she inadvertently did not pay her last insurance bill. She received her invoice in the mail, but forgot to send her payment.

Toward the end of the case, the prosecution makes a public announcement asking for anyone who was there to come forward and be questioned for information.

Jake and his mother are watching online, and when the prosecution made the announcement, Mom looks at Jake and says, "The Kenners!"

"Who?" asks Jake.

"You know, from Piscataway—Lillian and Tyrone Kenner, the people we were talking to when we were on TV," answers mom.

"Oh, yeah. What about them?" asks Jake.

"I bet they have not been interviewed," says Mother. "I am going to call them and tell them to call that information line number."

"You know something, that is a good idea," responds Jake. "I'll help you find their phone number."

Martha called the Kenners, and sure enough, they had not spoken to the authorities.

The second day of the hearing is very harsh on the Fischer family. The defense presents a sturdy case against the deceased, saying she should not have been carrying so many groceries and also, carrying such a big load for the family. She was burnt out from tirelessly working full days, and the fact that alcohol could have been involved makes the grandmother's ill-fated steps nearly understandable. The facts mount against Mrs. Fischer, and when lunchtime arrives, the prosecution knows they will get their final say in the afternoon.

When the courtroom reconvenes, the prosecution recalls two of the defense's witnesses, countering the defense's accusation of ignorance on the part of Mrs. Fisher. They also called on three character witnesses, who testified Mrs. Fischer had not had a drink for many years, and she was of sound mind. As two-thirty rolled around, Jake noticed the prosecution nervously checking the door and clock. Within minutes, the Kenners enter the courtroom, and the prosecution calls Lillian Kenner to the stand first.

"Tell us where you were and what you were doing when Mrs. Fischer was struck in the crosswalk," states the prosecution.

"My husband and I were sitting across the street having some coffee and a pastry, when we heard a loud thumping sound and loud screams. We looked up and saw the van turned sideways in the intersection and Mrs. Fischer's body lying in the street," says Mrs. Kenner.

"Did you hear the sounds of tires screeching?" asks the prosecutor.

Mrs. Kenner hesitates and looks toward her husband, and after a few seconds, she replies, "We heard tires screeching but the screech was definitely after the thumping sound."

"Are you sure?" asks the prosecutor.

"Yes. On the way home, we were both very wired with adrenaline, so we talked about it and recapped what happened. The screeching tires were after the loud thump," says Mrs. Kenner.

The prosecution calla Mr. Kenner to the stand and ask him basically the same questions.

At three o'clock, Judge Guyr tells the courtroom he will make a ruling at 9:00 a.m. tomorrow after hearing closing arguments. He also tells the court the press is free to interview whomever they please.

One interview of particular interest is with two of the Fischer grandchildren. The boy, Patrick, appears to be fifteen or sixteen, and is four of five years older than his sister Marilee Anne, who stands by her brother as he does the talking.

"Why do you think your grandmother deserves to be compensated for an accident where she is truly at fault?" asks the interviewer.

"We are not here to find that out. That is a different subject and trial, sir," says Patrick. "You do not understand what our grandmother was doing when she was killed, do you? Didn't you hear my aunt's testimony revealing grandma's schedule that day?"

"She was very difficult to understand from where I was standing. Regardless, why is that significant?" the reporter asks.

"Grandma was tireless and completely selfless. When she was hit, she was heading to her car in the parking garage across the street. She was on her way to daycare to pick up two of her great-grandchildren, and take them to their dance lessons by two-thirty. After she dropped them off, she was to go to the local recreation center and pick up three of my cousins and take them home. This was a slow day for her, because on some days, she does not get time for lunch. If she is not helping with the kids, she helps her daughters and daughter-in-law keep their houses clean," explains Patrick.

"Grandma never hurt a soul in her life. She loved life. She loved music and movies and laughter. We don't know what the heck she was thinking when she stepped off that curb, but God bless her soul." Patrick hesitates. "We miss her a lot."

"Did she gamble or drink?" asks the reporter.

"Why would you ask us that," demands an irritated Patrick.

"We hear she attends Alcoholics Anonymous," replies the reporter.

"My mom says she used to enjoy drinking, but that was over seven years ago," responds Patrick.

"Are you sure?" asks the reporter.

"Most definitely. I am sure of it," responds the boy.

Jake watches until the story is over, and then turns off the TV and goes for a walk outside. Jon and Tommy are shooting baskets, while mom and dad sit in the patio sipping fruit drinks and chatting. Jake walks over and sits between them on a chaise lounge.

"They just interviewed two of Mrs. Fischer's grandchildren, who said how loving and caring a person grandma was to everyone. Then the reporter grilled the boy about his grandmother being a drunk. I thought the kid was going to cry," says Jake. "The reporter was so relentless, it was brutal."

"Margaret was a drunk?" dad asks.

"I don't think so, at least not for many years. That stupid reporter just hounded that kid. Do you think it is a ploy or something to help Senator Jessport?' responds Jake.

"It could be," chimes in mother. "The press is ruthless you know."

"That is for sure, Mom," replies Jake.

"Are you going to watch tomorrow, Jake?" asks Mom.

"I would like to, but Pam and I are busy all day, so I will set the recorder," he answers. "Are you going to watch?"

"If I remember, I will," says mom.

Jake has an idea, so he heads to the computer room. Once on-line, he searches for information on Judge Guyr. He finds many links for Guyr, half of which are for Judge Thane Guyr.

Thane Guyr graduated from Harvard with honors over thirty years ago. He spent four years on a Federal Court during Ronald Reagan's term as president, and is now the chairman of the Eastern Judicial Association. In his search, Jake could not find anything negative or derogatory about Thane Guyr. He has led a normal, committed, unexciting life and displays solid knowledge and temperament.

Jake feels compelled to communicate with the judge in some manner or form. He looks online through Guyr's yearbook from his college days, and finds over a dozen pictures of the judge. Thane Guyr was plain and simple, but at least he smiled in most of the photos. There was one particular photo that caught Jake's attention. The photo was of Guyr and his soccer team, in a field of corn and pumpkins. They were having a good time, and Jake noticed the sweatshirt Gury was wearing had a picture of Lillian Gish on the front. Jake recognizes her from a silent movie festival the family checked out this summer. There was no mistaking Lillian Gish's face on Thane Guyr's sweater.

This gave Jake an idea. He wants to contact Judge Guyr to give him his own insight about the Fischer trial, but knows it is very difficult to be heard. So, he will send an e-mail to the judge. It took a while, but Jake finally found one of the Judge's e-mail addresses on line. There are quite a few addresses, which are very similar, but something tells him he has the right one when he finds it. The something is a combination of common sense and Purgatorial insight.

TO: Judge Guyr

SUBJECT: LILLIAN GISH LIVES

Judge Guyr, my name is Jake Martee. I am about to start my third year of college. *I am sending you this e-mail because I had a serious dream about you last night.*
I cannot tell you all the specifics about the dream, but I do remember this:
Pray tonight for clarity
There you have it. I am not sure if it means soul-searching, or possibly uncovering pertinent evidence in the Mrs. Fischer case.
All I know is the dream and waking up remembering the specifics.
I really do believe the dream to be relevant.
Thank you for reading this email.
Sincerely, God bless you.

Henry Jacob Martee
776 Spruce Avenue
Lincoln, Illinois, 62656

Jake says a short prayer out loud and clicks "send." He hopes his wishes will come true.

After a few hours, Jake is ready for sleep, and lying down on his bed never felt better.

———

Jake opens his eyes in his dream to see Oswaldo smiling at him. They are next to his house floating on the celestial platform, and immediately begin their journey for the golden gates of purgatory. Before long they make their way through the Arches and land on the Lobby, where Benjamin Franklin is waiting for them.

"Welcome, Jake, and thank you Oswaldo," says Ben as Oswaldo returns the gesture and then leaves the spot.

"Hi, Ben," says Jake. "What is up today?"

"Judge Guyr read your e-mail, and he sincerely prayed. You did a fantastic job, and thus far, we could not be happier. Of course, you know there was no way Judge Guyr was not going to read your e-mail, if we could help it. He did not hesitate when he saw that Lillian Gish was involved. Good thinking, my friend. Now, it is time for us to steer Judge Guyr's mind toward the right decision."

Ben's platform glides away from the Lobby and ascends past the Administrative Area to the Live G-A Hall. They come to rest at the doorway of Judge Guyr's Virmory.

"Jake, this is Gusto, Judge Guyr's Guardian Angel," says Ben.

"Pleased to meet you, Gusto," says Jake.

"Same to you, Jake. Welcome!" responds Gusto.

"Have you always been Judge Guyr's G-A?" asks Jake.

"Yes, since he was born," answers Gusto.

Ben interrupts, "Before we scurry to Thane's R-A-S, tell us about his Virmory."

"The Disclosure Wing has been rock steady for years. There are hardly any signs of wear and tear anywhere but the Gnostic Area. In the Gnostic Area, we found that his emotional communities have been scarred a bit from past cases and relationships, but everywhere else is bright and healthy. The L-S-S sent two dozen M-C-Us into his Amy-G to search for any type of evil presence or hormonal imbalance, and found that Judge Guyr is well intact. They also found the same results in the Brocal Area, and after one look at Tryphangle bridges, this judge is definitely not crooked or foul-mouthed," states Gusto.

"You know the Tryphus connection cannot be seen in the disclosure wing right?" Ben asks Jake, who nods in agreement. "We simply cannot take it for granted that it is operative—we have to make sure, otherwise our final efforts could turn out to be senseless. Believe me, we would take another route to influence Judge Guyr if his Limbic Highway had serious occupation."

Butch arrives in the Red M-C-U, so Ben and Jake glide aboard, leaving Gusto behind. They leave the Judge's virmory, meander their way to Thane's R-A-S, and come to a stop. Ben instructs Butch to bring on support, and within minutes, hundreds of green M-C-Us gather behind them.

"Cerebra is deemed ready. Are we ready, Butch?" asks Ben.

"Yes, sir," answers Butch.

"OK, we wait," says Ben.

"Why all the M-C-Us?" asks Jake. "I thought we are going to watch Judge Guyr's dream."

"We will Jake. For now we are not going anywhere until the dream begins. Most of the M-C-Us are going to the healing generator for dreamtime. The rest of them will stay with us to help in our endeavor," says Ben who takes a moment to browse the consoles.

Ben continues, "This episode offers a different twist than we are used to, Jake. Judge Guyr does not have obvious occupied sections that need serious cleansing, so we expect a successful transmission. The dream is expected to help him formulate a decision based on truth, facts, and common sense. Once the dream starts, any evil occupations hiding amongst the dead pools, will try to conglomerate and affect things, which could cause indecision or doubt in the Judge's assessment. We aim to be ready to stop any conglomeration. The power of the positive must be active for the Judge, thus, the preventative defense of having the M-C-Us standing by for cleaning and mending," finishes Ben.

The majority of green M-C-Us speed off into the Basal-G, vanishing into the Cable-Four. The Red M-C-U remains, and they are ready to watch the dreams cerebra has created for Judge Thane Guyr.

SIX

Judge Guyr's Dream

Thane Guyr looks around his old neighborhood. Nothing is as he remembers. There is a small strip mall where his grade school used to stand. The field where he played stickball and kicked the can is now a parking lot, surrounded by low-income housing. His favorite oak tree is long gone, and the memories of his first kiss blow in the wind. He is standing there, feeling nostalgic, when a fast-moving four-wheel drive truck comes to a skidding halt, right in front of the convenience store.

The convenience store is built right where home base of Thane's first baseball park used to sit.

A young man dressed in a flannel shirt and blue jeans gets out of the truck and spits tobacco juice on the ground. He goes in the store, comes out a few minutes later carrying a small white plastic bag, and gets back in his truck. A young, simply dressed lady, parked next to the truck, gets out of her car and goes into the store, returning with her purchase in hand a few moments later. She starts her car and pulls out of the parking space. As she proceeds toward the highway, the truck starts backing up and nearly hits her. She is so startled she blasts on the horn and yells at the truck driver. The truck stops just in time as she goes by, barely avoiding a fender bender.

The lady stops close enough to say something to the truck driver who is leaning his out the window.

"Why don't you watch where you're going, lady!" he says.

"Excuse me?" replies the lady. "You pulled out on me, dude. I was clearly in the right. Didn't you see me? Are you blind, dude?"

"Dude? You're calling me a blind dude?" says the brash truck driver. "Come on lady, get out of the car so we can discuss this face to face. That is if my blind ass can see you," responds the truck driver.

The lady now realizes she wants nothing to do with this frightening, threatening individual, so she quickly leaves the parking lot, with the truck swiftly following her lead. Less than a mile down the road, the car does a U-turn and heads back to the convenience store parking lot. Thane sees her pull into the same space where she parked before, just as the truck barrels up behind her, screeching to a halt. The lady stays in her car as the guy gets out of his truck. Thane sees an empty beer bottle roll off his floorboard, crashing to the ground.

The man walks up to the lady's car and vehemently yells at her, spitting all over her window. After several verbal threats, the guy gets in his truck and tears out of the parking lot, leaving clouds of burned rubber smoke lingering in the air.

The lady is obviously shaken up and sits in her car, both hands firmly gripped upon the steering wheel. Thane has watched the whole thing and cannot believe it. He walks up to her window and motions for her to open it. She opens it while hiding her face. Thane can tell she has been crying.

"Do you know that guy?" asks Thane.

"No. I have never seen him before," she says, still sobbing. "He said I deliberately pulled in front of him. Did you see anything?"

"I saw the whole thing. That individual is a loser. You are lucky he didn't harm you or smash your window, and I bet he would have if you were somewhere else, out of the public eye. It is a good thing you came back," says Thane. "Can I buy you a cup of coffee?"

"Sure, I could use one right now, or maybe a stiff drink," she replies with a somber chuckle.

They head into the little restaurant next to the convenience store for some coffee and conversation.

Before they enter the restaurant, Thane finds his dream is now at his dad's best friend Dave's house. Thane is there with his father Ted, Dave, and Dave's son Bear. Thane is twelve, going on thirteen, and he listens intently to the adult conversation. Thane scrutinizes everything he deems important or interesting, which is an excellent attribute of a good judgelike mind.

Dave is shooting pool, while Bear leans against the cement wall.

"You heard about Dix Frederick's kid, Johnny, didn't you?" Bear asks Ted.

"No, who is he?" replies Ted.

"Who was he is more like it," responds Bear. "He went to high school the same time I did, and was a real smart-ass trouble maker. Anyway, he was riding shotgun with his sister, taking an off-ramp on the freeway, when some guy cut them off. Johnny did not like that so he stuck his head out the window and yelled obscenities and flipped the driver off. Well, that didn't go over well, because the driver pulled a gun and shot Johnny dead. Fredericks was a smart-ass, but he didn't deserve to die. You simply should not say anything to anyone when you're on the road."

Thane is throwing darts at the wall, listening closely. He remembers hearing about Johnny being shot. His mother knows Johnny's mother from the quilting club, and Mrs. Fredericks was quite upset when the crime occurred.

"Bottom line is, the system needs to take the extra step to identify losers," says Bear. "I know it might sound far fetched, but what about some type of test check that raises a red flag and forces them to have a device in their vehicle, so when they are behind a wheel, the law will know. I know, it sounds obtrusive and possibly impossible, but what the heck—if something can be done to warn us about these criminals off the street, then why not?"

"I hear you, Bear," says Ted. "You just cannot trust anyone on the road."

Thane's dad breaks the rack of pool balls with a very loud crack, while Thane throws the last dart in his hand, and as he does, he drifts into a different scene of his dream. He finds himself in Philadelphia in 1788, standing on a wooden sidewalk filled with people. There are dozens of horses, and horses with buggies, bustling about the dirt streets. Two young ladies are talking when they start to cross the street. A fast-moving cart pulled by two horses approaches the ladies, but the driver cannot stop it, and the lady dressed in red is run over, killing her. Chaos ensues as the lady's friend, who avoided being hit, screams at the top of her lungs. Dozens of people run to the scene as the driver of the buggy hovers nearby, visibly shaken. Within minutes, two judicial-looking keepers of the peace take over the scene and direct people and traffic. After nearly four hours, the town turns back to normal.

Thane is following the crowd of people who are still abuzz because of the accident. There is an impromptu immediate hearing in the courthouse regarding whether the driver is negligent. The girl's father is really putting up a fuss about the how the driver should be charged for the accident. He thinks the driver was definitely going too fast to stop in time, and he feels the court is not taking the charge of negligence seriously. If he had been going slower, his daughter would be alive today, and he insists someone needs to pay for the injustice.

At the end of the hearing, the board rules the friend of the victim is going to be charged for illegal street entry, and no charges will be filed against the driver. The victim's father is enraged, and many of the onlookers are in disbelief. Alas, this was the ruling, and a trial will ensue.

Thane cannot believe what he witnessed at the hearing. The next thing he knows, he is in the courtroom for the last day of the trial. Benjamin Franklin is head counsel for the defendant. Franklin wanted the job, even though he is one of the most influential men in Philadelphia, not to mention the colonial United States. Benjamin Franklin never let an issue he felt was a steppingstone go unturned. After a day and a half of witnesses and deliberation, it was Ben's turn for the defense's final statement.

"Thank you your honor," begins Benjamin Franklin. "Ladies and gentlemen of the jury, the citizenship of Philadelphia, my fellow peers, I bid you all a good day. For two days we have listened to all the facts of this case, we have conceptually reviewed the incident as it truly occurred, and we have reviewed and considered similar instances. Let me say, as we venture into a brand new life as a country, we absolutely must set our priorities straight. We are all created equal, and we all deserve the same respect in a courtroom," says Franklin. "As we strive to make our laws the most prudent laws in the world, we must never lose sight of man and his roots. Transportation and artillery are going to continue to evolve, both will be stronger, faster and more efficient than you and I will ever be able to fathom. Contrary, man will always have only two legs when standing on his own. They are the same legs today, as he will have two hundred years from now. He will not get additional appendages, or become mechanical. Who is to say which transportation vehicle is too fast, too awkward, or too heavy to be on the road?

No one can say. All assisted transportation must be categorized as that, assisted transportation. No matter if it is a bicycle or a steam-powered machine, assisted transportation is different, and more dangerous than walking. If you keep this in mind, the pedestrian on foot, should always, one hundred percent of the time, have the right of way." Ben pauses, and adjusts his glasses. "How can it be any other way? If it takes a person twenty minutes to walk five thousand feet, and it takes a horse drawn carriage only thirty seconds to go the same distance, why should the person yield to the carriage in a controlled medium? Only in emergencies or dangerous situations, should the person yield.

We simply cannot afford to let our laws and courts fail to get out in front of the rules. If they do not, this will leave us in dangerous situations created by our own ignorance or laziness. The need for speed certainly does not outweigh the rights of the individual. Two hundred years from now, I hope our country never gets to the point where man coerces the court to make rulings based on the machine having more rights than the pedestrian." Ben takes a few seconds to look at the faces in the courtroom, "There is no possible way that poor girl would ever win against one, two, three, or any number of horses and buggies. Her rights were not protected, and we must use this as precedent. This untimely death of a vibrant young human being will be utilized to establish the principle that the pedestrian has the right of way. Finally, to avoid these terrible tragedies in the future, we must move in the direction to clearly identify and enforce pedestrian boundaries within city limits."

Benjamin Franklin, head counselor for the defense, scans the faces of the jury and the courtroom, and then says, "Thank you for your consideration."

The dead girl's friend was acquitted of any crime, and within ten days, the city of Philadelphia began employing guards to control traffic patterns at twenty of the city's busiest intersections. The driver of the buggy was not charged, but was fined five dollars for creating a nuisance.

———————

Back in Judge Guyr's R-A-S, Ben is all smiles.

"What do you think?" Ben asks Jake. "How did I do?"

Jake looks excitedly "Wow, Ben! You were hot!" answers Jake.

"Hot?" inquires Ben.

"Yes, awesome," replies Jake. "You were right on the nose. Judge Guyr will understand, right?"

"I think so, Jake. All of our research proves that Guyr is on the level. The only thing would be if large undetected evil occupations are wreaking havoc in his Limbic Highway. I surely do not think there is a remote possibility of that scenario, because we scoured his Highway pretty thoroughly. Alas, we will find out soon enough," says Ben.

"Is that all for the Judge?" asks Jake.

"From purgatory, that is all. Now, it is up to the Judge to sort through the facts, his dreams and his feelings," says Ben.

"What more can we do?" asks Jake.

"Gusto will keep track of the Judge's emotions from here, and the Judge will have to find the answers within the trial. Being able to be *certain* that Cerebra's dreams are absorbed by Judge Guyr, makes it worthwhile for all our efforts. If you had not been involved, Jake, we would not have been able to access and send M-C-Us to the affected areas of Judge Guyr's Healing Generator. Cerebra's dream could have very easily been ignored, or not even considered. This way Jake, we know for sure Thane's R-A-S 'played out the dream,'" says Ben. "It is simply fantastic, Jake, that we can utilize the L-S-S in someone else's R-A-S with your presence. I know we need to see the results before we get too excited, but so far, everything we have done with you has been successful. Why should our Creator send you here to do these things, if there is not a purpose? We are doing the right thing, Jake. Believe me, there is much more for us to accomplish."

"What is next?" asks Jake.

"Let us get out of here first. Take us back to Jake's Virmory, Butch," instructs Ben.

The Red M-C-U spins around and slides back into Jake's R-A-S. Butch takes them to Jake's Virmory. He drops them off and the Red M-C-U scurries away.

Ben and Jake float down to the lobby of purgatory. Today's work is now finished, as Judge Guyr has seen Cerebra's dream. Everything is in place.

"Thank you, Jake, I will see you sometime after the ruling. Take good care," says Ben.

"I will, sir. You too. Thank you for everything," replies Jake as Oswaldo whisks him away toward the planet Earth.

The next morning, Judge Guyr lies in bed scrutinizing the facts. He tries to leave his feelings out of his decision-making as he thinks of his recent dreams. "Road rage has hard bearing on lives, and is unfair to youth," he thinks to himself.

Later that morning at the courthouse, the crowd rises to its feet as Judge Guyr enters into the courtroom. "Good morning, ladies and gentlemen," opens Judge Guyr,

The courtroom sits and Judge Guyr begins, "I would like to hear final statements, after which we shall take a short break. Then I shall announce my decision. Mr. Prosecutor, are you ready?"

"Yes your honor," replies the attorney. "Anita Jessport was not paying attention and was in too much of a hurry to stop her delivery truck from hitting Margaret Fischer, causing her death. Sure, she had flowers to deliver, and a schedule to keep, as she is constantly trying to make good time. She is a young, bustling woman, who is caught up in this fast-paced society we have created. Witnesses testified she was wearing headphones when she got out of the van, and she appeared shocked to see what had happened. The fact she did not have active car insurance adds to her lack of character. We checked to see if there were reasons she might have inadvertently missed her insurance payment, and found that she has credit card debt, and has been late with many payments over the last two years."

The prosecuting attorney, pauses for a moment, takes a drink of water, and continues, "The daughter of a state senator does not have insurance. She claims her nonpayment was inadvertent, but the facts show she has been financially tight for two years.

Mrs. Fischer was none of this. Mrs. Fischer did have automobile insurance. She was a hard-working, tax-paying citizen her entire life, and she died while helping her children's overburdened families. It should not have ended this way for Mrs. Fischer. The facts speak for themselves, that even though Margaret Fischer made the wrong move stepping into the crosswalk that day, Anita Jessport was negligent in her driving. She was not paying attention when turning the corner at a busy intersection, and she did not have insurance. Margqret Fischer should be alive today!"

Judge Guyr acknowledges the prosecution, pauses for ten seconds, and turns his attention to Ms. Jessport's attorneys, "The defense may take the floor."

"Thank you your honor," says the attorney for the defense.

The head defense attorney straightens his tie after he stands, collecting his thoughts he prepares to begin.

"Anita Jessport is a diligent worker. She is never late for her job, does not call in sick, and has had not had complaints about her work. She wants to go to college someday soon, but has not decided on a career. She has never been arrested or done anything unlawful in her life other than a handful of minor traffic citations. Surely, she did not want to hit Mrs. Fischer on that midafternoon day. She just did not see Mrs. Fischer when Mrs. Fischer was entering the crosswalk," says the young attorney. "It really is as straightforward as it appears, and could have happened to any driver making that turn."

The lawyer puts his hands behind his back. "My client's only miscue that day, was to look left for a split second for traffic coming from the far lanes. In that split second, Mrs. Fischer basically stepped right in front of her. What happened? What prompted the elderly lady to step into the crosswalk? In fact, for all we know, Mrs. Fischer might have been drinking."

"I object your honor," says the prosecuting attorney as he rises to his feet. "This is out of context."

"Objection sustained," says the judge, obviously irritated. "Both of you please approach the bench."

"What the heck are you doing presenting hearsay in your final statement?" asks Judge Guyr. "Did the prosecutor know of this?"

"I heard the same thing last evening but I did not know the defense would mention the fact," answers the prosecution.

"I am quite shocked by the lack of concern for court procedure. This kind of malarkey often gets cases thrown out of court. It takes some nerve, young man, to stray from procedure, don't you think?" Judge Gury asks.

"I thought the information was pertinent," he replies. "I apologize."

"My goodness son, you must present your facts or opinions during daily procedure, or ask for a continuance. Do not you think you would have found out earlier if she had been drinking recently? To what kind of ethics do you adhere?" asks Judge Guyr. "Finish your closing remarks."

The defense is befuddled. "Yes your honor."

The two attorneys return to their tables, and the defense finishes. After the close, Judge Guyr addresses the court. "We will take a twenty-minute break, at which time I will render my decision."

Twenty minutes later, the court reconvenes, and Judge Guyr begins, "We need to keep our priorities straight in regards to the individual's rights inside the public transportation system. I thought for sure I would rule yesterday in favor of the accused, but when the couple from Piscataway testified, I began to see the world from Mrs. Fischer's eyes. How can anyone try to convince us that Mrs. Fischer is a bad lady in any form or sense of the word? There was not a bit of evidence that Mrs. Fischer had been drinking that day, yet unknown circumstances shoved her into that crosswalk and she was killed. However, there was evidence presented to prove that Mrs. Fischer was diligent and committed to her family. I will ask anyone on earth to show me how Mrs. Fischer was anything but absent-minded the day she died."

The Judge takes a short drink of water.

"What really happened?" the judge asks the court. "Think about it. There are two key facts of this case. The first is that Mrs. Fischer was a dedicated, caring grandmother who unknowingly stepped into a busy intersection. The second is that Ms. Jessport had many distractions while she was operating the delivery van, be it using her cell phone, listening to headphones, or looking at something across the road. The fact there was no screeching before she was hit proves Ms. Jessport hit the brakes after striking Mrs. Fischer. Anyway you look at it, the pedestrian deserves the right of way. There will be a jury trial, and it will begin this coming Monday morning."

The courtroom rises to its feet as the judge leaves the bench and enters his quarters. A heavy buzz fills the courtroom as people react to Judge Guyr's decision. Dozens of press people type information on their phones, and the Fischer family is smiling, at least for now.

Mrs. Martee is watching the proceeds with her son Jake. After the decision, she goes over and hugs her son.

"What did you do that for?" asks Jake.

"Why? Your mother cannot give her son a hug?" asks Mother.

"Of course you can, anytime," replies Jake.

"You are silly Jake. You like the results as much as I do," responds mother. "I very pleased with you and myself for encouraging the Kenner couple to make their court appearance. I think it made the difference."

"I agree, mother," responds Jake.

He thinks to himself, "And Lillian Gish!"

(5)

Jake cannot remember when he felt so good. Since the party at Blink's parents house, everything has been going well for him. Plus, he has four more days of summer vacation before going back to college. He is finished working his summer job, and has saved enough money to plan a move off campus after the first semester this fall. The previous ten days he has spent with his friends and family. Now, he gets to spend the last three days with Pamela. He has never slept better in his life, and wakes up wanting to search out problems and situations that interest him. It is a strange sensation for Jake to be like this, and he feels as though his enthusiasm might be overbearing. However, he tells himself to not get too wound up, because the last thing he wants to happen is, to ruin any chance he might have of getting lucky with Pamela before returning to college.

At midmorning, Jake uses the house phone and calls Pamela to confirm this evening's schedule.

"Good morning, Pamela! How did you sleep?" asks Jake.

"Great, honey! How about you" she replies.

"Excellent, thank you, It sure feels good to sleep in," answers Jake. "When did you get up?"

"A little before eight," says Pamela. "What are you having for breakfast?"

"Two soft boiled eggs with toast, a banana, and orange juice," replies Jake. "What about you?"

"I am having it right now. I have a bowl of peach yogurt with banana chunks, a half a piece of toast with chestnut butter, and a cup of cranberry tea. I wish you were here to enjoy it with me," says Pam.

"Yeah, me too," replies Jake. "Are we still on for tonight? We will go to Nick's for a pasta dinner, and then see that sci-fi movie we talked about."

"Yes, Jake, I look forward to it," says Pam.

"I'll pick you up at six, OK?" asks Jake.

"Yes, that's fine," replies Pamela. "What's wrong with you today? You seem jittery. Have you been drinking coffee?"

"No coffee for me. I have just been pumped up lately. You feel it too, don't you? I mean, you are done with your summer job, you have a little time off before heading back to school, and well, by golly gee Pam, you have me to play with for three days!" remarks Jake.

"Easy, big boy. We get only three days, and then you are gone. It is difficult to get overexcited because it will go too fast," elaborates Pam. "See you tonight."

"See you then. Bye, Pam," voices Jake.

The rest of the morning and entire afternoon goes fast. After Mother tells them to, Jake and Jan clean their rooms entirely. Jan painted her room two weeks ago, so her job was simple. Jake has a much more detailed task, and by the time he is finished, his shirt is soaked with sweat and it is time to start getting ready for his date.

After a shave and a shower, Jake goes downstairs to join the family. Jon is home from school, and Mom is in the kitchen preparing dinner while Jan is on the computer. Dad walks in the front door, home from work.

"Hello everyone, I'm home!" proclaims Mr. Martee.

Little Jon runs out of the kitchen and greets his father.

"How was your day today, daddy?" asks Jon.

"Great. How was yours?" replies dad.

"Not too bad. I can't believe we've been in school for two weeks already. Do you have to work tomorrow?" asks Little Jon.

"No, Jon-Jon, I am caught up at work and have the entire weekend free. Do you have a game tomorrow?" asks dad.

"I do. We're playing at the naval housing field. You've been there a bunch of times," says Jon.

"I know the field. What time is the game?" asks dad.

"Eleven in the morning. Are you coming to watch?" asks Jon.

"Your mom and I will be there. Who are you playing?" asks dad.

"We are playing the Whiparounds. This is their first year, but they're pretty good. They beat us five to one at the start of the season," says Jon.

"Something smells good," says Dad as he strokes Little Jon's head on the way through the kitchen door.

"Hello, Mother," says Dad, "How the heck are you today?"

Mom turns at him with a surprised look.

"Aren't we looking happy today? What's going on?" asks mother.

"Nothing, really. I am just happy it is the weekend," says dad. "Aren't you?"

"Of course I am, darling. This is a big weekend for our family. Just think— two summers from now, Little Jon will also be going off to school. Then, we'll be home alone," says Mother.

"Sounds exciting!" says Dad, with raised eyebrows.

"Be quiet," says Mother in a much lower voice.

"Smells like corned beef, Mother," says John.

"It has been cooking since before lunch, Here, try a bite," Mom says as she spears a small piece of corned beef and puts it in his mouth.

Dad blows cool air on the hot piece of meat and puts it in his mouth, "Mmm, perfect," he says. "Let's have a drink."

"You go ahead. None for me," replies Mother.

Mom stands by the stove while Dad is pouring himself a beverage as Jake walks in the kitchen.

"Where are you going all spiffed up?" asks Dad.

"Pam and I are going to Nick's for dinner, and then we'll see a movie," replies Jake.

"Nick's eh? Excellent choice! Do you know what you're going to have?" asks Dad.

"Pam is going to have some type of linguine and I am going to have cheese ravioli. I'm hungry though, and I cannot wait to eat," conveys Jake. "The evening can't get here fast enough."

"Love takes time," declares Dad. "If you start to get nervous, just remember to appreciate the fact you are in the moment."

John Martee did not realize that what he said means a lot. Jake is hoping to make love to Pam before they go back to college, and he always feels his brain and heart race when he thinks about it. Even though neither one of them is a virgin, the two of them have talked only a few times about going all the way.

Pamela went out with Derek Trestling her entire senior year of high school. She told Jake they made love twice. There are many opportunities at college for a female as good-looking as Pam, but she just isn't into it like some of the other girls. She wants to stay focused on school and make something of all the money her parents and she will spend. Pam likes a couple of guys in college, but she knows that if she gets too mixed up with them, her scholastics will suffer. Plus, she is not into casual sex. She and Jake have been going out since last Christmas, and she is happy with their relationship.

Pam first went out with Jake their junior year in high school, when they went to a school dance together. She liked him, but they did not go out again. In the summer of that year, Derek started dating Pam. They established a relationship, which lasted until Thanksgiving of Pam's freshman year at college.

On the other hand, all of Jake's friends and family heard about Jake losing his virginity. After it happened, Jake was very embarrassed about it at, but after a few months, the embarrassment wore off.

It was July, in the summer after Jake, Kevin, and Gregg graduated from high school. They wanted to grab life by the horns before entering college, so the three of them took a road trip to Nevada. Jake and Kevin ended up spending their money somewhere in the middle of nowhere, at a place called the "Sage Bush." Greg had a girlfriend at the time, so he abstained.

Kevin met a white girl from Nevada, whereas Jake's first experience was with a skinny girl from Thailand. When they got back to town, word got around of what they had done, and everyone kidded the two of them until they left for college. It bothered Jake a lot because he is shy about girls and love. He also felt ashamed because he knows deep down the best thing in the world is to be in love. He does not want to treat it like a game or business. Kevin maintained it did not bother him, but Jake knew he was bothered as well. Still, it happened, and eventually, Jake felt kind of good about doing it before going to college. It took the peer pressure of making love for the first time out of the picture. However, Mr. Martee explained to Jake that the first time is very special, and to remember this in the future.

Jake and Pam had started going out after seeing each other at a party during Christmas break the past school year. The rest of the year they talked or e-mailed each other nearly every day, and would send a surprise through regular mail at least once a month. Their relationship remained steady the past summer, but never achieved "lover" status. Now, it is the last weekend before going back to school, and Jake is hoping something happens between them that has never happened before.

Jake leaves the house as the rest of the family sits down for their Friday dinner deluxe. When he gets to Pam's house, he takes five deep breaths to help keep him calm as he knocks on her door.

"Hi, Jake," says Pamela's mother when she opens the door. "Please, come in. How are your folks? Do tell them hi for us."

"Hello Mrs. Norris. Mom and Dad are well—thank you for asking—and I will definitely tell them hello," replies Jake.

"I'll tell Pam you are here. Make yourself at home," says Pamela's mother.

Jake follows Mrs. Norris into the living room where Mr. Norris is reading a magazine. The evening news is on the television.

"Honey, say hi to Jake," Mrs. Norris tells her husband before she leaves the room.

Mr. Norris gets up and shakes Jake's hand. "How are you doing, Jake?" Mr. Norris asks. "Are you ready for another year?"

"Yes sir, I believe I am ready. For what, I do not know," replies Jake with a chuckle.

"I have heard about you. Pamela says you are a good student and a nice guy. Keep up the good work. You have to get any edge you can nowadays. My pops survived the Great Depression of the early thirties and he used to tell me stories, which sound too similar to what is going on today. I mean, I think you are definitely going to survive, but you young people are going to have it tough. Keep the nose to the grindstone and it will pay off," finishes Mr. Norris.

"Yes, sir, I will for sure," responds Jake. "Are you taking Pam to school next week?"

"Yes, her mother and I will drive her. I look forward to seeing that part of the country this time of year," says Mr. Norris. "The colors are always fantastic."

Pamela arrives at the doorway and motions for Jake to come join her.

"We're going, Daddy. Don't wait up," Pam says to her father.

Pam's father gets up again and shakes Jake's hand while her mother stands in the hallway behind the couple.

"What time should we expect you?" asks Mother.

Pam looks at Jake and smiles, "Jake?"

"Oh," says Jake. "We will be back before midnight."

"Have a good time," says Mrs. Norris. "I will leave the back porch door open and the light on for you."

"Thanks, Mother," replies Pam. "Bye."

"Goodnight, Mrs. Norris," says Jake. "It was very nice to see you."

Jake and Pam lightly converse about her parents on the way to the restaurant. They laugh when they talk about how serious her father acts.

Nick's restaurant is packed. Fortunately, Jake made reservations a week ago, so they are able to walk right past the long line of hungry people waiting at the entrance. Inside, they are seated at a cozy table along the back wall.

During dinner, they talk and talk about many things. Pam admits she is happy the two-day camp-out at the Owens cabin fell through. She told Jake she was nervous about being alone together for two whole days and nights. She told him she is not ready. Staying at home and doing things together is much more relaxing and enjoyable than camping ninety miles away. Jake agrees with her, but hearing what she says gives him the feeling that his inner desires might be put on hold.

The dinner finishes with a small plate of fruit surrounded by two streaming circles of chocolate butterscotch glaze. Jake uses his debit card to pay for dinner and then pulls Pam's chair back as she gets up from the table. They comfortably get to the car and make their way to the movie house.

The movie is good for both of them. It is a science fiction story with a lighter comedic flair. They both laughed out loud more than once during the film. In the parking lot after the movie, they solidify their plans for Saturday and kiss for a minute or so. They will drive to the lake in the morning, and attend the party at Greg's house after dinner.

Jake drops Pam off at her house just after eleven-thirty. He walks her to the back porch stairs, and they exchange a long hug and short kiss.

"See you in the morning, Jake," says Pam. "Thanks for the pleasant evening."

"Thank you. Good night, Pamela," says a smiling Jake as Pam walks up the stairs.

Jake waits by the car door until Pam gets into the house, and then gets in the car and shuts the door.

While driving home he says out loud, "That was a great evening."

All is quiet in the house when Jake gets home. He brushes his teeth and hits the hay.

Before falling asleep, Jake thinks about his family and friends and all kinds of different relationships. He wonders about Pamela and her friends. He wants to make love more than anything, but she appears to be holding back. He feels he deserves it but knows this thinking is a messed-up attitude, which would not go over well if he mentioned it. But, does he press the issue, or should he be feeble and wait until later, at school, or whenever?

"Is that being weak?" he asks himself. "The guys would all press on to make something happen, especially if they get their girl to drink," Jake conjectures. "What are the right things to say? When is the right time to make the move? Where do we go? Why am I so insecure, and why does it bother me?"

He takes a few deep breaths to push the worries from his thoughts, and falls asleep.

Jake does not realize it, but his insecurity has allowed evil barbs to find their way into the emotion sections of his Gnostic Area.

The next day, Jake picks Pam up at 8:00 a.m. and they drive for nearly an hour to Lake Hebo for a morning of hiking followed by a picnic lunch.

Their nature hike is a blend of fresh air, rustling leaves, and many varieties of bird song. They toss breadcrumbs to the ducks at the lake, and throw pinecones at each other until Pam gets mad at Jake for hitting her in the face with one.

A sudden rain squall cleanses the air and briefly interrupts the normal forest noise. They find a tree with a canopy to protect them from the rain, which enables them to hold each other tight until the passing weather calms.

For lunch, they find the cleanest picnic table in the park and make a nice arrangement to enjoy. Lunch consists of cold fried chicken, crisp apple-carrot salad, celery sticks, pretzel twists, and grainy oat rolls. Pam brought a Thermos of iced tea to accompany the food.

After lunch, they pack everything in the car, take one final deep breath of fresh air, and enjoy one last hug before leaving. On the way home, they confirm their plans for the evening. Jake will pick Pam up after dinner around seven, and they will go to Greg's house for a summer-ending party among friends.

During the drive home, when they are not talking, Jake thinks about the right things to say to get Pam to make love with him before going back to school. He loves her and wants to do the right thing. He knows from experience that saying something wrong, can have more of a lasting effect than not saying anything. He has always puts his foot in his mouth when it comes to girls. But, he figures if he doesn't say anything, he surely will not get anywhere. At least, that is what he thinks.

Jake turns off the car when they get to her driveway, and asks, "What do you think Pam? Should we get a room somewhere tonight?"

"Are you serious? Does this mean you're going to pay me like that beyatch in Nevada?" Pam sternly replies, obviously irritated.

"No, it is not like that. I love you and will love you forever," falters Jake.

"Really, Jake?" questions Pam. "If that is the case, what is the hurry? Do you have to have this way? My goodness, honey, I thought you are more mature."

"What are you talking about?" asks Jake.

"Think about it Jake. Think about how you implied it, like you are *telling* me in advance. I don't like it!" says Pam as she gets out of the car.

Jake is choked with fear and adrenaline. He can tell he has screwed up. "I'll see you at seven,"

"Whatever. I'll be ready," responds Pam.

As he leaves the Norris residence, he knows he almost blew the chance to take Pamela to Greg's party. He is so glad to hear her say she will be ready.

"I am such an idiot," he says to himself on the way home.

———————

"What is it, Allyson?" Ben asks Jake's G-A.

"Jake's Gnostic Area is showing some excessive brightness, and we can deduct sputtering along the Appurvesti. You wanted to know if there is ever any suspect activity? Well, this is definitely some suspicious activity," explains Allyson.

"What are your frets?" asks Ben.

"Jake appears to be flustered. He has occupancy because he is displaying mild signs of temper and rage. Pam is not giving in to his sexual wants, and he is confused," says Allyson.

"I am coming over immediately," states Ben.

Before Allyson can say anything, Franklin arrives at her door.

"Besides the trembling Appurvesti, the Disclosure Wing shows signs of disturbance around the Amy-G where it enters the P-F-L. This, in turn, emits bright streaks scattered in the upper portions of his Gnostic Areas."

"Is the L-S-S checking the Tryphangles?" asks Ben.

"Yes sir. They have been there for over three hours. So far we have not spotted any tainted connections. They are also scouring the Healing Generator to find any leads," explains Allyson.

A few minutes go by, and Allyson elaborates, "Here is the report. You are correct, Mr. Franklin."

Ben and Allyson observe Jake's reader board and see certain sections of the Gnostic Area are lackluster, showing signs of occupation. It is hard to say how much occupation, but there is definitely something there. "Some of the connections between the Amy-G to the temper sections in the Gnostic Area are also sputtering." says Allyson.

"The L-S-S has taken control and sent two or three hundred M-C-Us to guard the Gnostic Area. When the timing is right, we must attack to avoid further penetration, even if we are not exact. The M-C-Us at the Amy-G and the P-F-L, need to wait and not attack, because if we do attack, evil barbs could possibly penetrate deep into these cognizant zones to avoid early expulsion. This will allow heavier, deeper neuron consumption than we wish to allow. So for now, we will be waiting and ready," explains Ben. "We must be very cautious tonight. Pam and he are going to the summer's end party, which means there will be alcohol and temptations, which could lead to some dangerous situations. His confidence is shaken, proven by the obvious barb presence. Hopefully he will not do anything too peculiar or wrong, because the worst results would be to have him disconnected from our Purgatorial relationship."

"Be careful and thorough, Allyson," adds Ben. "The L-S-S has as many M-C-Us as you need. Keep him covered."

"Yes, sir," replies Allyson. "What if I cannot keep up?"

"Do not worry Allyson; the L-S-S is on your side. Just do your job, and everything will be all right."

Ben knows it is not as simple as what he told Allyson. The unknown implications of Jake's involvement with purgatory, worries him, the Fathers and Leaders, and all of Cerebra. They are all concerned because they know that Jake is a human, who can be influenced like anyone during strenuous, momentous times, especially if alcohol is involved. The thought of losing the bond between Jake and purgatory looms large.

Fortunately, there is no direct evidence that evil senses Jake's presence in the Limbic Highway. If and when evil barbs do catch wind of Jake's newborn existence inside the Limbic System, the frenzy they can create is potentially dangerous. However, because evil is cunning but not smart, it may never become aware of Jake's Limbic attendance. Jake is protected when Limbic traveling except when he is in a vulnerable part of the system, such as when the Red M-C-U is roaming the Cable-Four of the Limbic Highway. Allyson will monitor the hundreds of M–C-Us guarding Jake's Gnostic Area and Amy-G. Even though there is no way to watch all the Tryphus connections, the M-C-U patrols will at least give the L-S-S early detection notice.

Thus far, there is no way for evil to detect his presence.

———

Jake cannot make it to Jon's soccer match because of the picnic, but Jan was able to join her parents just before halftime. The score was 1-1 at the break, but the opposition scored two goals in the second half to win 3-1. After the game, Jon rides with his sister, and they caravan behind Mom and Dad back to the house. Jake got home twenty minutes earlier and made a jug of iced tea for the family. Mom and Jan make sandwiches for a late lunch, while Jon showers upstairs. Dad and Jake watch college football on the television in the living room.

"How was your picnic with Pamela?" Dad asks Jake.

"It was very nice. Hardly anyone out there, and there wasn't any wind, just a minor rain squall. We should have had our fishing poles," says Jake.

"They rent poles at the lodge," says Dad.

"I know, but we had a good time anyway," responds Jake.

Little Jon enters the living room and tells the guys lunch is ready. They all make their way to the dining room table and sit down for chicken salad sandwiches, corn chips, and pickles. Jakes only consumes half a sandwich, some chips, and a glass of iced tea, since he enjoyed a picnic lunch with Pamela only a few hours earlier. After their lunch, Mom and Jan do the kitchen work while the guys go back to the living room.

"What are you and Pam doing tonight," Dad asks Jake.

"Greg is having a summer-ending party at his folks' house. Everyone is going up there to have some fun. Man, his folks' house is so nice. It's huge," elaborates Jake.

"Are you driving home?" asks Dad.

"If I don't drink, I will drive. Otherwise, Kevin is the designated driver, and we'll leave our cars at Greg's house. We will see how that works out," replies Jake.

"Are you going to drink?" asks Dad.

"I might have one or two. Pam says she doesn't want to drink tonight, so I probably won't either," answers Jake.

"Do you think you'll get into Pam's pants if she doesn't drink?" Little Jon surprisingly asks.

"Little *Jon!*" says Mother standing in the living room doorway. "Where did that come from? My goodness, you need to watch your mouth."

"You're funny, little bro," says Jake. "I can only hope."

Jake tries to not look bothered by his brother's rhetoric, but the issue is on his mind and the mention of it brings to surface his nervous feelings.

"What's wrong Jake? Hasn't she been giving it up?" continues the badgering Little Jon.

"For gosh sakes, Jon," says Jan as she sits on an easy chair, "You act like it's a game or something."

"Be nice to your brother, Jon," says dad. "Women are difficult enough to figure out without you making fun of the situation. Plus, you'll get yours someday. Have you forgotten how you felt after Jeannie dumped you at the start of the summer?"

"She was a Scrooge, anyway," remarks Little Jon. "I'm sorry, Jake. Tonight is your last night, so go for it!"

"When do you ask your girlfriend if you can kiss her, Jon? Before or after she chugs a soda pop?" asks Dad while he laughs out loud.

"Ha-ha, Dad. It's weird, but they ask me. Well, my current friend and I haven't kissed yet, but we've only known each less than two weeks. The last girl kissed me first. Really! I love it!" spouts Jon.

"Can you believe this guy?" Dad asks Jake. "You would think he has a halo on the top of his head. It just goes to show you, we are all blessed with different attributes."

"He is lucky," says Jake, trying to downplay his own role in the situation.

"Things will work out for you Jake. Use that brain God gave you and things will be OK," Dad reassures Jake. "Don't fret about it."

Jake goes upstairs to check his college preparations, and to be alone. He double-checks his closet to make sure he has packed what he needs for Monday's departure and then lies down on his bed for a short rest. As he lies there, he thinks of his little brother's luck with girls. "What does Little Jon have that I don't?" he asks himself.

Jake has never asked Little Jon if has made love yet, and he sometimes wonders. They rarely talk about the parameters of love. In fact, Jake only talks with Kevin and Greg about love. Mom and Dad had a talk with Jan and himself in junior high about the birds and the bees, but since then, Dad has never directly addressed love issues with Jake.

Jake believes in love. However, he is having a tough time connecting his strong feelings for Pam with the desire to make love. And, he is having an even tougher time communicating any of this with her. He knows are all the facets are connected, but the pressure from society has put undue demands on his view of premarital sex. He is confused by the demands because he overvalues peer approval in regard to what is truly best for him. Pamela's values are solid, and she trusts herself in confidence.

Twenty minutes later, Jake wakes up from his short nap to the sound of the neighbor's lawn mower. His head feels a bit weighty from the sleep. He gets up and stretches his arms to the ceiling and thinks of Pamela. He convinces himself he is going to have fun tonight, regardless of the outcome. Jake showers and cleans up, and then goes downstairs dressed in sweat pants and a tee shirt. He can smell au jus cooking as he walks into the kitchen.

"Au jus, my absolute favorite. You're the best mother," says a jovial Jake. "Do we have ridges as well?"

"Yes Jake, two bags," replies mother. "Did you take a nap?"

"I did get a short snooze in, and it sure helped," answers Jake.

After Jan arrives, they all sit down to dinner.

The kids know Dad is going to say the dinner prayer tonight before dinner. He always does for important meals, and this last Saturday night together as a family is an important meal.

John Martee speaks aloud.

"Dear Lord, thank you for this food Mother has prepared. We hope everyone in the world gets something to eat today. Thank you for a healthy, loving family and many good friends.

We pray for safety and success for our children during their upcoming travels and endeavors in college and adulthood. Thank you for everything you do for us. Amen."

"Amen," everyone responds.

Dinner is under way, and they all dig in at the same time. Jake smiles to himself while he looks at each and every member of his family. Dad is always in a good mood, especially tonight, during an office-free weekend. Mother is diligent in her daily tasks of running the family. She stays busy every day, but once in a while, she still enjoys a game show, a soap opera, or an hour-long detective show on television. Staying busy keeps her healthy. Little Jon is the spoiled little brother of Jake and Jan. He always seems to be "up" at school and at home. Girls like Jon, and he is very popular at school. His grades could improve, but he has close to a B average, which will get him into any of a number of schools within driving distance from his home. He has two more years of high school to maintain or improve his marks.

Jan is the eldest of the Martee children. Being the oldest has given her a sense of responsibility, and she exemplifies such an attitude. Besides guiding her brothers to good study habits, she is always willing to help around the house or do favors for anyone. She is strong-willed and on the right road to becoming a doctor of pharmacy. She has been going out with George for two months, but does not want to think about marriage until after she becomes a pharmacist.

After dinner, dessert, and dishes, George picks up Jan for the evening. Jan tells Jake she will probably see him later at Greg's party, after they go to the esplanade. Little Jon prepares to watch a movie with his mother and father in the living room.

Jake gets dressed and says his good-byes to the family and leaves to pick up Pam.

By the time he gets to Pamela's house, it is nearly eight o'clock. Pam answers the door and yells to her mother she is leaving. Pamela leads the way to the car. There is not a whole lot of conversation on the way to Greg's house, and Jake can sense Pam is still upset because of what he said earlier in the day.

They are pleased to find there are not too many people at the party—not like the crowd at the Owens party five weeks earlier. The house is nice and warm as the guys hang out at a table by the kitchen, milling about, playing cards, and drinking bottled beer. The girls are in the living room. Most of them are drinking a mixed fruit punch, which Greg's brother Andrew concocted. The punch consists of fruit juice, lime soda, orange slices, ice, and grain alcohol.

The music gets louder by the song, and before long, there is dancing in the living room. Jake is playing cards, but keeps an eye on what is going on elsewhere. He sees Pamela is drinking punch, so he decides to have a few beers. The party is fun and before long, Jake realizes they have been there nearly three hours and the house is crowded. By midnight, the crowd begins to disperse. However, Jake cannot find Kevin, the designated driver.

'Where did Kevin go?" Jake asks his sister Jan when he sees her.

"I think he took off with the Yager girl. You saw her—kind of dark skinned, wearing a white puffy top showing her shoulders.," answers Jan.

"Oh yeah, she's cute," says Jake. "Darn that Kevin, he was going to drive us home."

"You can ride with us. We're leaving right now," states Jan.

"No, that's OK. We are going to leave after a while. We'll be just fine," replies Jake.

"Are you sure?" asks Jan.

"Positive. Don't worry about us," answers Jake.

By twelve-thirty, most everyone has found their way out of the house. Jake helps Greg clean up a bit while Pamela sits on the couch, talking with Greg's girlfriend Marie. Jake can hear her slur her words while she talks.

Greg already told Jake he can stay in his brother's room. Putting two and two together, Jake envisions possible sexual success.

Jake brings two glasses of water to the table and sits next to Pam on the couch. Marie goes into the kitchen where Greg is cleaning.

Jake thinks to himself, "This could be the perfect opportunity to put the blast on Pam."

"Thanks for the water, honey," says Pam with bleary, drunken eyes.

"You are very welcome, my dear," replies Jake. "Let's go rest for a while in the other room."

"Sure, Jakey. What do you want to do? Fool around, you nasty boy?" says Pam.

"Why not? We are not going to see each other for quite a while," he replies.

Fortunately for Jake, the hint of dominance in Jake's last sentence did not register with Pam.

Pam gets up first and grabs Jake's hand, "C'mon honey. I need to lie down."

Jake gets up, but Pamela falls at the same time. She hits her shin on the table and says, "Damn! Oh well, just another scar."

Jake steadies her and they saunter into Andrew's bedroom. He turns on the light to check out the surroundings. There are car racing posters and framed pictures on the wall, and the room looks and smells clean. He turns out the light, and they plop onto the bed and begin kissing passionately.

Jake tries hard to keep his senses and make the correct moves. He fondles Pam's breast while they kiss, and then makes his move to unbutton her jeans. She pulls his hand away and puts it back up to her breast. He enjoys the feel of her upper body while continuing to kiss her. After a few minutes, Jake tries again to unbutton her jeans. Pam has been loving and jovial, but this time she stops and tells Jake, "No!"

After a few more moments of rising sexual intensity, Jake does not want to stop. However, Pamela is losing her ability to resist and is ready to pass out. Jake continues to move on. He gets her jeans button undone and starts to slide his hand down her pants. Suddenly, he thinks he hears her snoring and finds she is indeed asleep.

———

"What's going on, Allyson?" asks Ben.

"Jake's Amy-G is off its rocker—it looks like a neon bonfire! The M-C-U patrols have found infected areas along the bridges near known secreting areas. Somewhere there is concentrated suffocating barb occupation attempting to coerce Jake to be cruel. Evil is trying to hinder his conscience and allow his mind a guilt-free mind-set of continuing on, even though Pamela told him to stop," says Allyson. "Their purpose is to convince him he deserves to continue."

"For goodness' sake Allyson!" cries Ben. "Love is such a fickle aspect of life, yet it is the key to the core of our existence. We cannot let this happen. It could sever Jake from purgatory, so make sure you are involved at all times."

Butch shows up immediately. "Get moving, Butch," says Ben. "There is not a second to waste, and where is the back-up?"

"They will meet us in Jake's R-A-S, Mr. Franklin," responds Butch.

Ben slides onto the M-C-U, and they whisk into the R-A-S. Waiting for them there are two hundred M-C-Us.

"The Tryphus is close to getting cut off at the connecting bridge to the Amy-G. If it does, Jake could seriously violate Pamela's rights," Ben says to Allyson and Butch.

"Darn it, Jake. He knows better—what is he thinking?" asks Ben out loud.

"There are so many bridges, how can we pinpoint the ones in question?" asks Butch.

"If we get lucky, we can get a bit of a read from the Tryphus itself," says Ben.

Butch leads the entourage into the P-F-L. After a few minutes of travel, a few dozen green M-C-Us veer off to the sides, swerving in and out of neural communities to expand the search.

As they approach the Amy-G, pathways begin to brighten, and then darken. The whole atmosphere is breathing, much like the rhythm of an ocean wave, and their Red M-C-U is swaying left and right, while it bobs up and down. Looking closely at the brightest tracks, they can see certain areas where the Tryphus bridges are being attacked.

"Look!" exclaims Ben. "We can see where it is happening. Wait right here."

Butch slows to a slight roll and mingles among the Tryphus bridges adjacent to the Amy-G, their vessel continuing its carnival-ride motion.

"Now is the time. We have to move quickly," decrees Ben.

Ben hastily adjusts his console and brings up Pamela's Virmory on the screen. Sabina, Pamela's G-A, appears and addresses Ben.

"Yes, Mr. Franklin. What is your suggestion?" asks Pamela's G-A.

"Do something to shake up her Gnostic Area. Pam must fight off Jake before it is too late. Pamela has got to be the answer to saving Jake from falling out of Purgatorial grace. Get it done Sabina," demands Ben.

"You got it, Mr. Ben," replies an enthusiastic Sabina.

———

Jake is becoming very aggressive. Pamela had been enjoying their exchange, but she is losing the joy and energy of the moment, and now she is falling asleep. As he makes his way down the front of her jeans, she snaps out of her delirium and slaps Jake hard across the face.

"You're a bastard. What do you think you're doing?" she cries.

"Gee whiz, Pam, what are you doing? Aren't you enjoying yourself?" Jake asks mischievously.

"Gee whiz," she mocks. "I was enjoying myself, but now I don't know what the heck you're doing. Is this the way you want it?" asks Pam, barely keeping her eyes open.

He does not want to take no for an answer, and as he sees her eyelids sag into sleep, he considers his next move.

———

"Did you see that?" Ben asks Butch.

"Yes, sir, we did indeed," replies Butch.

In no time, Butch and over two hundred M-C-Us speed to the edge of the Tryphus to Amy-G connections. The slap on the face has lit up the infected bridges enough to allow Butch and the crew to hastily set up shop and cleanse thousands of evil barbs off Jake's Highway. Afterward, Allyson reports to Ben.

"The Amy-G is starting to simmer down. The throbbing light is subsiding. This will help, right?" she asks.

"Sure looks like it," replies Ben. "But we are not out of the woods yet, by any means. Keep a close eye on the areas around the repaired bridges. We could have missed an evil colony or two. We cannot let him slip away from his healthiness."

"Yes, sir," responds Allyson.

———

Pamela cannot stay awake anymore. She loosens her grip on Jake's arm and falls back on the pillow.

Jake is about to continue, but the force from her slap still stings and both-ers him inside. He suddenly finds himself shaking his head, wondering what made him act so crudely, so unrefined.

"I am not like this," he tells himself. "This is too weird. This is not like it is supposed to be. What the heck am I thinking?"

Now, he does not hesitate to do the right thing. Pam is passed out and he could take advantage of her if he wants to, but his conscience rises to the occa-sion and sets his values straight.

"I need to be there for her, not take advantage of her. How can I expect to be loved the way a man wants and needs to be loved, if I cannot love that way myself?"

Jake listens to his surroundings. It sounds like everyone is gone. The only noise he hears are voices on the television. He tries to wake Pam so they can get up and leave Greg's house, but she is sound asleep. Jake buttons her jeans and blouse, picks her up, takes her to the living room, and lays her on the couch. He goes to the kitchen, finds some instant coffee, and pours water in a pan to boil. After the water is ready, he pours two small cups, adds some milk, and goes back to Pam. He sits and watches her while he drinks his coffee; she is in no shape to indulge. After a few minutes, he puts her jacket around her shoulders and carries her out to the car. She is heavy, but he handles her gently and easily; his summer workouts have proven beneficial.

Jake always keeps a blanket in the back seat of his car, and he places it over Pamela to keep her warm. He leaves the windows open the entire drive home. He figures the hot coffee and the cold breeze will do him good to drive sober. When they arrive at Pam's house, he surprisingly has little problem waking her from her stupor. He helps her get out of the car, and they slowly wobble their way to the back stairs, with Jake supporting her the whole way. They make it to the top of the stairs, and he opens the doors and walks her into the back porch. He makes sure she is aware of what is going on and gets ready to leave.

"I love you, Pamela," he whispers in her ear. "I will call you tomorrow."

Pamela rolls her eyes at him and replies, "You better, you big lug."

With this, Jake heads home. Pamela has survived a night of excessive drinking, which she will pay for the next morning with an excruciating hangover. She has also survived nearly being improperly advanced upon by her boyfriend, but all is good because she knows inside that the right things happened.

When Jake hits the hay, he falls asleep as soon as his head hits the pillow.

—

Ben Franklin and all of Cerebra are relieved Jake is safe. However, they are not sure how this experience will effect Jake's Limbic affiliation. Ben knows Jake did the right thing and that getting a dream to register will confirm Jake's connection with purgatory is intact.

—

Jake is watching from his dream as young John Martee and Martha Martin set up for a picnic under a maple tree in the middle of large, rolling meadows. The two of them are enjoying a beautiful country day. Their picnic basket is filled with sandwiches, crackers, cut-up pieces of vegetables and fruit, and beverages. After their lunch, the two of them lie on the blanket, cuddling and contemplating their lives. They laugh and giggle while talking about anything and everything.

Martha is glowing and very beautiful, and Jake sees that the two of them are happy. After a bit John sits up and reaches into the pack he brought. He pulls out two roses protected by plastic. One is bright yellow; the other, deep red.

"Martha Jean, we are so lucky we have found each other. It makes me tingle every time I think about us," says John as he repositions himself on the blanket.

He reaches out, takes Martha's hands and calmly pulls her up to a sitting position.

"Will you marry me, Martha Jean?" asks a very nervous John as he shows Martha an engagement ring nestled in a soft blue velour ring box. "Please?"

Martha is surprised and speechless. She does not want to answer immediately and starts to cry. In the meantime, John is getting nervous as no answer has been spoken. He wants to speak again, but remembers the financial sales tapes he listened to his first year of college. The part of the tapes he is thinking of is when the speaker says, "After your final sales pitch, remember one thing: The first one to speak loses." The statement lingers in his brain, so he waits.

Finally, after drying her tears, Martha speaks, "Oh, John, I must be dreaming, because I have always wanted to be a part of a beautiful story, and now I feel we are one of those stories ourselves. *Yes!* The answer is *yes, yes, yes!*"

They hug for what seems like ten minutes, and exchange many warm kisses. John wipes away the tears from Martha's eyes, and then his own, and says, "I have a short tune I wrote for us, honey. Would you like to listen to a verse or two?" he asks.

"Please my love, please," she says.

I always know my dreams are alive
When I see the beauty of the Hawaiian Islands
One plus one, plus two plus two
Can recharge even the weak
Then suddenly, you appeared
My restless feelings fade away
Morning sun, the mountain caps
Make me feel brand new, 'cause

Love is a union of God and our spirits
I can feel you inside
You will now become my beloved bride
Why can't the world feel like we do
Where everyone is on everyone's side
Thinking ahead to eternity
While enjoying every stride, cause
Love is a union of God and our spirits
Tough times will be all right
You shall now become my cherished bride

———

Jake is standing next to Ben Franklin in the lobby of purgatory.

"Welcome back, my boy. For a short while I thought we were going to lose you because your libido almost got the best of us. Thank goodness your presence in the Limbic System is masked to keep evil from knowing your status. Did you enjoy seeing your mother and father become engaged?"

"That was awesome, Ben. Thank you for that," answers Jake. "It is *great* to see you! What happened last night? I know Pamela made it home safely, as did I, but before we got home, the last thing I remember is almost violating her after she passed out. I am so glad I did not go any further. Did you have anything to do with my stopping?"

"It surely did not hurt that we kept your Amy-G somewhat mellow. Additionally, Pamela's G-A, Sabina, stimulated her, or should I say assisted her, with the slap to your face. You remember the slap to your face, don't you Jake?" Ben asks somewhat as a matter of fact.

"Of course I do, Ben," answers Jake.

"The slap revealed the location of fluttering bridges between the Tryphus and Amy-G. Then, Butch and the boys cleansed most of the occupations immediately. Also, you made the right move Jake, because you are who you are. And, because you are here, all is good," explains Ben.

Ben continues, "The dream of your parents' engagement you witnessed was created by Cerebra and solidifies the connection between love and peace. Your mother and father are prime examples of family strength within the Limbic System. Your folks are still together and happy after twenty-five years. The percentage of marriages lasting longer than ten years has dramatically dwindled in a relatively short period of time. The moral strength of family and marriage remains solid, but, the numbers of families, parents, and couples without this intangible cohesion, has increased exponentially.

"Additionally, the lesson for you is that true, honest love is a mutual feeling. You were on the verge of breaking that bond," says Ben. "The breaking of that bond might have broken our bond, but thank goodness, we are here talking. We are extremely relieved you survived the validation."

'Is it going to happen again?" asks Jake. "I was so close to doing a bad thing. There are so many temptations and tasks to deal with in life. The last thing I want to do is jeopardize what we have here."

"We are going to talk in the halls of Cerebra about the situation. You really have the place buzzing, Jake. There is a council waiting for me now, and I will let you know what we all talk about the next time you visit us. OK?" asks Ben.

"OK, Ben," replies Jake. "What is next for us, do you know?"

"We are not sure yet, but the ultimate goal is for love, happiness and peaceful times to dominate the earth. I know it sounds unfathomable, but two months ago, who would have ever believed you would know Allyson and me?" asks Ben.

Ben hesitates. He knows he might not see Jake for a while, as the college atmosphere will more than likely keep Jake extremely occupied. He puts his arm around Jake and looks over his glasses into Jake's eyes. "The future of America and the world can be influenced by you, Jake," says Ben. "Forty years from now, your country—excuse me, *our* country—will be bankrupt unless nations unite as a whole. If the balance of power shifts to communistic or terroristic ideas, earth will have a difficult time sustaining human presence. This scenario is one we will do anything and everything possible to avoid. Your presence in purgatory is the first step to saving the earth, Mr. Jake. As usual, the timing of our Creator is impeccable."

"I am totally excited and committed," replies Jake. "When do we get started?"

"My boy, you are so genuine and somewhat naïve. We began the first moment you went through the magnificent gates of purgatory," replies a somewhat jovial, yet humble Benjamin Franklin. "I will tell you this, however; you have learned of the individual Limbic Highway of man. Next up will be learning the details of evil's presence."

"Wow! OK, Ben. I will be ready," replies Jake.

The two of them exchange a solid Purgatorial hug and bid adieu.

Oswaldo arrives and Jake glides onto his platform. They heartily salute Ben as they swoosh away, off to planet earth.

Later, Ben steers his platform in the direction of Cerebra. He knows the council is prepared and waiting for him, yet is relieved the way things worked out the way they did. If they had lost Jake, this upcoming meeting would be grim rather than positive.

Ben arrives at the meeting hall to a council of twenty.

They are seated in the middle floor of a six level terrace. Today, the head figure is Alexander Hamilton. Surrounding him are Sophocles and Aristotle on his left, while Thomas Jefferson and Martin Luther King flank him to the right. The rest of the council is comprised of significant figures of the past, sitting at the opposite end of the virtual table.

Hamilton speaks. "Welcome, Benjamin. We are ecstatic that young Jake is still with us. You understand the importance of his affiliation with the Limbic System, don't you? What on earth happened that we came so close to losing him?"

"Good day to you sir, Alexander Hamilton and all you ladies and gentlemen," replies Ben. "Of course I understand his affiliation. I am shocked to hear your tone of voice."

"Jake has just discovered purgatory and he already walks the edge? This is not what we anticipated," says Hamilton severely.

"Come on Alexander, what did you anticipate—world peace in a day, or an end to world hunger? You know as well as I, this is brand new to purgatory. My friends, experience is the best learning tool. This is Life. Life is all about experiencing the intangibles. That is how God created the world. Otherwise, life is too obvious to decipher, with no expectations," elaborates Ben.

"And his near violation?" asks Hamilton.

"We were tested, but we succeeded," responds Ben. "This was a difficult but worthy test of the system as evil went right to their best opportunity, the intangibles of love. The slap exposed the dangerous infected areas, enabling the L-S-S to assist in solving the mystery. We learned a lot today, and for now, we are going to be OK."

"The council feels that Jake might be sketchy and could lose the connection at any time," says Hamilton.

"You have got to be joking. You all witnessed the results. What are you going to do? Replace him? Have you forgotten how WE lived our lives? I will be the last to point fingers at any of you. But, I will be the first to point a finger at myself. Jake showed a weakness in the love department, the intangible, emotional love department. He is only human, you know." Ben stops for a few seconds then continues, "Look at me. I loved women my whole life. I loved French women beyond description, and ruined the best relationship in my life because of my infidelity. Yet, here I am. Maybe the fact we both ethically struggle with love, is why I am Jake's mentor. We all know the mystery love's emotions offer life and the Limbic Highway."

Ben hesitates and looks at each individual seated at the great table, waiting for any reply.

"Additionally, I must admit, this shared trait might be our only bad trait," Ben says smugly. "Give us a break. We were tested and we succeeded. Obviously, the future continues to have hope!"

The council has no rebuttal, only agreement and thanks. There are no sure things in life, but as usual, common sense reigns supreme. Alexander Hamilton, Benjamin Franklin, and the rest of the Cerebral council stay in discussion for over an hour.

Finally, after the Halls of Cerebra have cooled, everyone is back to his or her business. Ben is back in his residence in the Father's tier. He reviews the last six weeks of the Limbic System with Jake involved, while occasionally gazing over the top of his glasses at the expanse of purgatory. He thinks of the future and all that Jake will learn of the earth's atmosphere, and smiles.

The first thing Jake thinks about when he wakes up is how ashamed and stupid he feels. Stupid, because he drank alcohol then drove a motor vehicle. He feels ashamed because he came close to violating his girlfriend. For twenty minutes he lies awake, thinking about the entire day, from feeding the ducks to helping Pam stagger up the back stairs to her home.

After deliberating, Jake tells himself he is very lucky he avoided trouble last night, and he will definitely avoid putting himself in similar situations in the future.

He feels something deep inside himself that he feels is pure goodness. Suddenly, he feels the biggest grin come over him, and he laughs to himself out loud. He sits up on his bed, and then gets up and walks over to the mirror on the wall. He scratches his head and rubs his eyes. He gets real close to the mirror and stares at himself.

"Jake, old boy, life offers many different scenarios," he says to himself, still looking into his own eyes. "Do not forget, old boy—and it will take sharp wit to always be on your game—that during intense moments, you must always find the time to think on your feet."

He stretches his arms as high as he can, and then reaches down and touches his toes. After ten repetitions, he looks closely at himself again and says out loud, "You know Jakester? Something inside you is making me feel we *can* make a difference!"

GLOSSARY

AMY-G: The endocrine hub of man's system
- Located in the lower exterior portion of the P-F-L
- Composed of massive complex purplish blue nucleus fields
- In conjunction with the thyroid gland, coordinates stimulation of 90 percent of the human body's hormones
- Plays major adrenaline role
- The Amy-G is buffered by the Appurvesti.
- Female labor and ovulation as well as human libido are regulated in the Amy-G.

APPURVESTI: The mental buffer
- Located in the Hypo-Bulbo
- Assists in the balancing of mental equilibrium by not letting the momentum of emotions within the Highway exceed its capacities or not meet its minimums.
- Works to buffer the Gnostic Area and the Amy-G to avoid tempers and emotions easily getting out of control

----

AUTONOMIC:
- To operate and function automatically, nonaffected by free will
- There are two autonomic cables of the Cable-Four, the Bellum and the Hypo-Bulbo.

BASAL-G: The voice of man
- One of the two cognizant cables of the Cable-Four
- Composed of large neural clumps and fields, separated within the community
- Speech is formulated in the Brocal area of the Basal-G. It then passes through the Thalamus to the Gnostic Area where the information is scrutinized, before returning back to the Brocal Area, where actual talking is initiated.
- Houses the Somaesthetic Area of the five senses
- Home of the Physical-4 nucleus, which helps maintain muscle control, balance bodily equilibrium, and regulate conscious and subconscious movements
- Home of the Healing Generator of man

BELLUM: The collecting house of information
- One of the two autonomic cables of the Cable-Four
- Located in the back, bottom area of the brain
- Composed of large dense neural trunks that collect all the information entering the brain
- Works closely with the Motrex to disperse the information with the proper amount of energy to its destination
- The Surface Modalities mechanism is harbored here
- Home of the Damping Effect
- Home of the Disclosure Wing

BROCAL AREA:
- Located in the Basal-G of the Cable-Four in between sections of the Somaesthetic Area, up against the Thalamus
- Speech is formulated here.

CABLE-FOUR:
- The four information cables of the Limbic Highway
- Travels from purgatory to man's brain
- The four cables are as follows:
  1. Bellum—autonomic
  2. Hypo-Bulbo—autonomic
  3. Basal-G—Cognizant
  4. Prio-Frontal Lobe (PFL)–cognizant
- All four cables are vulnerable to evil barb attack once inside the earth's atmosphere.

CAUDATE:
- One of the Physical-4
- Concerned in overall control of body movements
- Coordinates the timing of physical conscious and subconscious movements

----

CEREBRA: Home of the Dream Machine
- The top half of Cerebra is in immortal heaven. The bottom half is the uppermost region of purgatory.
- A vast gathering of facts and memories, utilized to scrutinize present and past situations in hope of helping the living
- Cerebra's information tracts intertwine throughout purgatory, enabling everyone accessibility as necessary.

CEREBRAL CORTEX: The signal sender
- Inner layer of the two outermost layers of the outer brain, the Limbic/Cerebral Cortex.
- Reads and scrutinizes all information, and then directs it to its proper destination in the Limbic Highway.

COGNIZANT:
- Pertaining to the two cognizant cables of the Cable-Four, the Basal-G and the P-F-L
- Cognizant means the cables are utilized and affected by man's thoughts and will

----

DAMPING:
- Located in the Bellum of the Cable-Four
- Monitors feedback of physical motion
- Prevents muscles from overextending
- Enables movement to be smooth instead of jerky

DEADPOOLS:

- Deadpools occur on the Limbic Highway, inside the Cable-Four.
- They form when the L-S-S has no alternative but to isolate evil occupation within neural pools, enclosing them within an impenetrable area.
- Evil barbs often hide and live among exterior boundaries of dead pools.

DISCLOSURE WING: Virmory's readerboard

- Located in the Bellum quadrant of the Virmory
- The Disclosure Wing emits an instantaneous current Limbic Highway status.

EVIL BARBS:

- The menacing, voracious substance and existence of evil, made of souls who do not go to purgatory
- The barbs attach and feed on the vulnerable sections of the Limbic Highway. They try to devour neuron to neuron and penetrate the deepest fissures of man's brain, where evil achieves its ultimate goal—the untimely death of a human.

EVIL BULGE:

- When evil takes over with enough mass to force the L-S-S off the Highway, and pushes its way to the deepest fissures of the brain, where it wreaks havoc with man
- A successful evil bulge predominantly ends in untimely human death or catastrophe.

G-5
- Shaped like an hourglass, a vacuum machine that sucks evil barbs off the Limbic Highway and spews them into the earth's atmosphere

----

G-A: Guardian Angel
- Everyone has his or her own G-A, which is located in a Virmory in the "Live G-A Hall" of purgatory.
- The G-A monitors a human's Virmory 24-7, and detects incongruities in the Disclosure Wing, which in turn utilizes the L-S-S to locate and mend occupied and damaged areas

----

GLOBUS P:
- One of the Physical-4 located in the Basal-G.
- Coordinator of background muscles and relaxing

GNOSTIC AREA: The Conscience of Man
- Located in the center of the P-F-L
- Sensitive monitoring area of talking, where moods and behavioral patterns affect what we say, and how we speak
- Speech, thoughts and actions are scrutinized and reorganized in the Gnostic Area.

HEALING GENERATOR: The power of the positive
- Located in the heart of the Basal-G
- Connected in some form to all of the Limbic Highway, thus enabling positive energy flow throughout
- The Healing Generator supplies positive healing energy to the pertinent area when prompted by thinking or prayer, or influenced by the L-S-S. It relies on the "power of the positive" to operate.

HYPO-BULBO: The coordinating area
- One of the two autonomic cables of the Cable-Four.
- Coordinates the cardiovascular and metabolic functions
- Regulates body fluids, body temperature, and breathing rhythm
- Houses the Appurvesti, which buffers mental balance

L-C-U: Limbic Cleansing Unit
- The automated evil barb cleansing unit, located in the outer layer of the Limbic/Cerebral Cortex
- The L-C-U is a fully automated, five-dimensional, gyrating, vacuum expulsing machine, which sucks evil barbs off the Limbic Highway as information enters the brain through the Cable-Four.
- The gyrating mechanism within the L-C-U is referred to as a G-5

LIMBIC CORTEX:

- The Limbic/Cerebral Cortex is the outermost two-layered section of the brain.
- The entrance of the Limbic Highway into the brain
- Composed mostly of 5-G barb removers

LIMBIC HIGHWAY: The road of life

- The celestial connection of man's brain to his guardian angel in purgatory, whose main function is to protect man from evil

LIMBIC SYSTEM:

- The elaborate, intricate, virtual support and protection system of reality, designed to help man survive and exist
- Consist of the universe, mortal and immortal heaven, purgatory, outer space, the earth's atmosphere, earth and man
- The Limbic System is the inner being of man.

L-S-S: Limbic Security System

- The anti-evil security system of the universe
- Created to protect the human internally, by monitoring his mind and body and then seeking out and removing evil presence
- The work force consists of L-C-Us, M-C-Us, participating G-As, and all working souls

----

M-C-U: Mobile Cleansing Unit
- The mobile security vehicle of the Limbic Security System utilized by the L-S-S to extradite evil occupations among neural pools and communities
- Designed to win Limbic battles by undisputedly removing evil barbs off the Limbic Highway
- Skippered by one or more G-A quality souls
- Equipped with 5-G barb removal units

MEDULLA:
- Located at the base of the Thalamus, in between the Pons and the spinal cord
- The massive nerve-ending center, which monitors and regulates the connection from the Thalamus to the spinal cord

----

MOTREX: The power source
- The rechargeable power source of man and the Limbic Highway, located at the base of the Thalamus, above the Pons.
- Works in unison with the Bellum to energize the entire Limbic System

----

NONVULNERABLE:
- Areas of the Limbic Highway where evil cannot adhere, enter or influence.

P-F-L: Prio-Frontal Lobe
- One of the two cognizant lobes of the Cable-Four
- Located in the upper, frontal section of the brain
- Composed of multiple folds of gray matter, allowing for rationalizing and human behaviorisms and free will
- Home of the Gnostic Area and the Amy-G
- The P-F-L is where some of the deepest fissures of man's brain exist, making it the favorite target of evil barbs.

PHUSSED:
- Occurs when the Tryphus is ignored or tricked into dormancy.
- The Tryphus will not put up with the deceit or mistrust of an area, so the bridge and connections close. This forces the information to travel a different route, usually against the grain of the Thalamus.
- Being phussed causes the system to lose energy.

PHYSICAL 4: the nucleus of physical equilibrium
- The four segments located in the Basal-G combine to coordinate bodily movements.
- They are as follows:
  1. Globus P
  2. Putamen
  3. Caudate
  4. Sub-Thalamic

PLATFORM:
- The main mode of transportation inside the communities of purgatory
- Equipped with a virtual ultrahigh definition console
- Travels only within the celestial walls of purgatory

PONS: the buffer
- Located between the medulla and the motrex
- Heavy, fibrous buffering area, designed to harness nerve speed and direction from getting out of control.

PUTAMEN:
- One of the Physical 4 movement nuclei, located in the Basal-G.
- Coordinates delicate movements, such as finger dexterity.

R-A-S: the Reticular Activating System
- Located in the heart of the Thalamus, above the Motrex
- Dreams and wakefulness are enabled in the R-A-S.
- The L-S-S gathers in the R-A-S, enabling quick access to the Cable-Four.

SOMAESTHETIC AREA:
- Located in the Basal-G, against the wall of the Thalamus
- Houses the coordination of the five senses

SUBTHALAMIC:
- One of the Physical-4, located in the Basal-G
- Aids in balance and physical equilibrium during bodily movement such as dancing, walking and jumping

----

SURFACE MODALITIES:
- Located throughout the skin of a human
- Sensations of the skin are interpreted and monitored to initiate particular functions of the brain.

THALAMUS: The control center
- Centrally located throughout the brain
- Nonvulnerable throughout
- The Thalamus scrutinizes all information as it enters the brain, for validity and direction.

TRYPHANGLE:
- An area in the brain where two segments interact with each other, while utilizing the Tryphus to measure truth and strength
- There are two Tryphangles:
    - A) Amy-G to Appurvesti to Tryphus.
    - B) Gnostic to Appurvesti to Tryphus

TRYPHUS: The Truth Meter
- The invisible intangible sheath surrounding the entire Limbic Highway of each individual
- The Tryphus acts on its own, and randomly tests any or all information for strength of truth.
- The more deceit and lies in a person's system, the less the Tryphus is utilized, and the less effectively it operates.

VIRMORY: Home of the G-A
- The Virmory is the cubicle in the Live G-A Hall of purgatory where a human's Guardian Angel resides.
- The G-A monitors the human's systems from the Virmory.

VULNERABLE:
- Susceptible to evil attack
- Any area of the Limbic Highway that evil barbs are able to occupy is termed vulnerable.

WORKING SOULS:

- Within the Limbic Highway, Working Souls are primarily utilized as soldiers aboard an M-C-U.
- Some of these souls are not suitable to be a G-A, because they have exhibited general laziness and ineptness in life, thus, they are not capable of Guardian Angel duties.

www.ingramcontent.com/pod-product-compliance
Lightning Source LLC
Chambersburg PA
CBHW060824120626
46557CB00001B/354